I0623881

# Echoes From the Past

## A Paranormal Mystery

## K. Francis Ryan

## Penman House Publishing

Penman House Publishing

Copyright © 2016 Roxann K. Brooks

The moral right of the author has been asserted.

All rights reserved.
No part of this publication may be reproduced, stored in a retrieval system, or transmitted, in any form or by any means, without the prior permission in writing of the publisher, nor be otherwise circulated in any form of binding or cover other than that in which it is published and without a similar condition including this condition being imposed on the subsequent purchaser.

Published by Penman House Publishing

ISBN: 978-0-9908764-7-2

Typesetting services by BOOKOW.COM

# In Memoriam

Jean Mace

A bright light that will continue to burn forever in the lives she touched with a gentle grace, a warm heart and a giving spirit.

* * *

# Acknowledgements

Although a solitary profession, writing is not a lonely one. A wealth of people is instrumental in the making of a book.

Many thanks go to my fellow Penman House authors: Christopher Clarke, Aaron Aalborg, Michael Crump and Riley Smythe.

An immense debt of gratitude is owed to my editor, Vanessa Warren.

The cover art was provided by Alexandre Rito. The man is a true artistic wizard with an uncanny ability to read minds. You can find him at: alexandre@designbookcover.pt

*** 

*A very special acknowledgment is due, and a debt owed, to Roxann.*

*Without her, doing what I love would not be possible.*

*She believes in me, especially when I do not.*

***

# Chapter One

Terrance Patrick Manning never entered the Irish Republic. The body count would prove it.

After its two-hour flight from Zürich, the elegant Gulfstream G200 taxied to a stop beside the customs station at Dublin International airport. Twin Rolls Royce jet engines continued to turn to deafening effect.

One man, tall, older and heavyset with iron gray hair, in an impeccably tailored dark suit, descended from the airplane. Baggage in hand, he awaited the immigration bureau official who walked from the station.

"Mr. Manning," the man shouted over the engine noise. "I am Detective Sergeant O'Brian. I'm afraid you must come with me. You are to be held on a Red Notice from Interpol. This way, sir," the official said.

"I would suggest you call for some assistance," Manning said. "There is a problem on the aircraft. The crew is dead. I'll wait here while you check." The gravity of the situation etched clearly on his face, deepening the lines around Manning's gray eyes.

The detective sergeant spoke into his radio and two members of An Garda Síochána, the Irish national police service, bolted from the building at a run. O'Brian instructed the officers to wait with Manning while he conducted an inspection of the Gulfstream.

As he entered, O'Brian found a female flight attendant sitting strapped to her seat in the crew compartment. Her head lolled to one side at an acute angle. Warm, but she had no pulse. The official opened the cockpit door and found the two pilots also dead. He began a check of the rest of the craft looking into closets and pushing aside drapes.

"That's not right," the official said to himself as he looked into the aft stateroom. "The manifest said three crew and one passenger," he whispered. In a leather recliner sat a tall, older, heavyset man with iron gray hair and an impeccably tailored suit. Dead.

The fire that erupted in the stateroom melted Detective Sergeant O'Brian's lungs in an instant. He died as he fell.

White hot flames trickled through the fuselage exploding windows as they went. The two waiting policemen radioed for help as they raced to the gangway to rescue their colleague. As they boarded the craft, blast-furnace hot flames engulfed the interior of the airplane incinerating them instantaneously.

Sirens and alarms sounded as fire equipment began moving toward the raging aircraft fire.

Manning turned and his concerned look vanished. He smiled slightly and walked toward a discreetly parked limousine. The vehicle proceeded at a dignified pace and evaporated into the Irish night.

* * *

"They say it is not the fall so much as the sudden stop that makes jumping off cliffs a great deal less enjoyable Julian," Bridget Bragonier said to the man whom she mentored and who she called her friend. She looked over the cliff's edge at the churning sea below and shivered with the cold.

Julian Blessing stood, balanced inches from a cliff edge, facing the Irish Sea. His shoulders were tense, but his hands hung relaxed, open and slightly away from his sides. The wind lashed at his clothing, straining its power to send him tumbling to the rocks and surf beneath him. His shirt snapped like a flag in a gale and the blowing salt spray sliced into the gaunt and pale skin on his face.

He wanted the pain, sought out the punishment, but felt it not at all. He stood unmoving and unmovable, suffering in a world caged by his own mind. His world was populated with acrid recrimination as the deaths he knew he caused played back to him in an endless loop of accusation.

Nature saves its darkest weather for costal Ireland's late afternoon. Soot colored clouds gusted across the Irish Sea from Great Britain. Rain threatened but obstinately refused to fall, preferring instead to menace and torment the Irish population.

The day was, like most winter days, cheerless. It had been this way on this spot of land for hundreds, perhaps thousands of years. Perhaps since the beginning, before there were years to count.

On a lonely spit of land, a man stood on its cliffs' edge and thought of a dark and painful past. But the land and the cliff, the sea and the wind never noticed. Nature doesn't take note of the insignificant, and one man in pain is manifestly insignificant.

In his early forties, Julian was a handsome man with brown hair blending into gray. Although once of an athletic build, he had become slight. Little sleep gave him an unnatural sallowness. A scar down his right cheek accentuated his lean features. He was tall and Bridget had to look up.

Julian's hands dropped back to his sides and he opened his eyes.

"I don't think I'll step off the edge today," Julian whispered. "Maybe tomorrow. You are here for a reason Bridget, or were you just in the neighborhood?" he asked the older woman.

Bridget was a tall, slim woman with silver hair and kind gray eyes. Her age was indeterminate – older, but certainly not old. More than beautiful, she was compelling. People were drawn to her by the sheer force of her presence. One of those people had been Julian Blessing.

The sarcasm rolled off her. "Mr. Manning is in the country. He covered his tracks well. I only found out this afternoon. Initially, it was believed he had been killed in an explosion in Rome. That was not the case. It was said he died in a fire a week ago at the airport. Both fitting ends to be sure, but sadly such was also not the case. He is apparently quite alive and he will most assuredly be looking for you. Or more to the point, he will be looking for what you have," Bridget said.

"That he is here doesn't surprise me. That it took you so long to discover does. My guess is he is obscuring his future moves from those with the second sight like you. He did it effectively in Rome. It doesn't surprise me he would do it here.

"By the way, Bridget," Julian said in a raspy whisper. "Please remind me again, what is it I have?"

"I cannot say precisely and apparently, you are not about to tell me. I would say that is because you are obstinate and truculent, not to mention cheeky, but I am too much a lady to say so," Bridget said and smiled her most charming smile.

"What you have is whatever led to the reported exponential growth in your talents, so it is easy to see why Manning would be interested in it and thus, in you. Doubtless you have a plan of some sort," she said.

"My plan is to stay here at the monastery. I see no reason Manning has to work very hard to find me. Here I am. Come or don't. I don't really care," Julian said.

"This is not like you," Bridget said with concern in her voice. The fine networks of lines at the corners of her eyes were pinched in thought.

"Nothing about me is like me anymore," Julian said.

"And when he comes for you, what will you do then?" Bridget asked.

Julian's forehead creased in concentration. He closed his eyes and took a deep breath. "Bridget, I am tired of the violence and death in the name of a just cause. I am tired of the light and the dark. I want out, out of this life. I am tired of the two worlds, tired of all of it."

As he said it, he knew it wasn't possible. He looked over the edge and fixed his gaze on a rock outcropping on the cliff face below. He held his hand out and the rocks shuddered then exploded. The superheated fragments tumbled down, hissing as they sank into the sea far below.

Bridget ached inside for her friend. She ached for what he had been through. She ached for what he would yet have to endure.

"Julian, know I would take your suffering away from you if I could. I will not minimize the pain you are enduring now. I comprehend it too well. Please understand too, what you want is unattainable. You have seen the two worlds. There is no way you can dismiss that.

"In many ways, your past dictates your future. The life you want to return to is no longer available to you. What happened to you in Rome changed you in some ways, but certainly not all. You must forge a new life. Use all your experiences, past and present, to create a life worthy of you," Bridget said.

"If my future is wedded to my recent past, I might as well step off the edge right now and save myself the trouble," Julian said with pain etched into his face. "Sounds pathetic, no?"

"In a word, no. I am, however, glad you used the word recent because not all of your past is recent, Julian. You had a life in New York before you heard the echoes. You have a life here and a place you can call home. You have friends who respect and admire you. You have Ailís, a woman who loves you with all that is within her. All of that is part of who you are too," Bridget said.

The wind gusted and Julian staggered, but maintained his position. The weak sun was setting and a dark day was edging into night.

"We will not resolve this today. We will not resolve this at all," Bridget said, stressing the 'we'. "This is something you must come to grips with. This is something you must do and soon. Let us leave that for now. I came here to talk to you about something else.

"There is a man, a teacher of mine from many years ago. He has asked to see you. He feels it is crucial he talk with you. Will you agree to meet with him?" Bridget asked.

Julian paused before turning to face his mentor. "I read the signatures of others; I get a sense of them. I've never known you to slip so badly, Bridget. Is there something about me that has you rattled? You see, you gave it all away. First, you already told him I would talk with him. Second, he was coming regardless of what either of us said. Third, because it is you who asked, I will listen to the man. I can promise no more than that," Julian said in his featureless whisper.

The wind and salt spray bit at both Bridget and Julian, making it hard to think but easy to feel. Bridget said, gathering her coat more tightly around her, "You may need to suffer, Julian, but I do not. I'm going in."

The corner of Julian's mouth lifted slightly. It was what passed for a smile and that thought saddened him and clouded his gray eyes. So much had changed unalterably.

\* \* \*

A bulky manila envelope landed on the sergeant's desk, heavily enough to push some other envelopes to the floor. The sergeant scowled and had to get out of his chair and under his desk to retrieve the last one. If not for that one letter, he would be dead.

The letter bomb in the manila envelope went off prematurely, causing a cascade of events and consequences that rocked the Garda Síochána's headquarters in Phoenix Park, Dublin.

In the nanosecond preceding the actual explosion, it was as if the building took a breath and held it before exhaling and blowing out all the windows on the first floor. Ceiling tiles fell, loose papers were caught up in the ensuing wind storm and members of the Gardaí were thrown to the floor or across the room. Car alarms and automatic sprinklers went off and everywhere the cries of those injured or trapped were answered by those able enough to rescue them.

The sergeant huddled under his desk grasping one small envelope. It was misaddressed. Fate is funny that way sometimes.

✳ ✳ ✳

"John, come in me boy. What brings you to my little bit of Ireland? I wish I'd known you were coming," the older man said with a jovial Irish inflection in his voice.

"In fact with your many talents, you did know I would be coming the moment I knew of your pursuit of the Book, of course. I might add, you knew I would come here first. By the way, what are we calling you these days?" said John Clarke, a tall, slim, impeccably dressed man in his forties with unforgiving gray eyes and a smile without feeling. His language was crisp and clipped and had perfect British public school modulation.

The older man considered a moment. "Terrance Manning, will do." He seemed genuinely puzzled. "I've called myself so many things over the years, it is sometimes hard to remember.

"I rather liked Terrance Cardinal Patrick Manning, but I suppose that simply won't do. The Curia isn't likely to welcome me back. Embezzle a billion dollars from the Vatican bank and they lose their sense of humor. Let's just go with Terrance Manning for now. So tell me, what are you planning to do?"

"Must we always play this game?" Clarke's voice bordered on boredom. "I'm here for the same reason you want me here. The Jesuit Book. We want it and you, at least, feel sure Blessing has it. I have three questions that are more important though.

"Is there any evidence he does have the Book and do you think he knows?" John Clarke's voice was usually languid tending toward boredom, but there was an edge, an undercurrent of malice now. "Where you are, I mean. Do you think he knows?"

"Thirdly, when will he come for you?" Clarke asked his mentor.

The heavyset older man with iron gray hair and eyes to match sat in a leather club chair before a crackling wood fire. "As to the first, he most assuredly did have it, but has since passed it off for safekeeping. It is the sort of thing he would never trust out of his possession to just anyone, so that narrows the search.

"Where it is, isn't important though. We need the Book, yes, but we need him more. He is an asset worth having.

"Addressing your second question," Manning folded his hands in his lap and looked at Clarke, the man who would eventually kill him and take his place as he had killed his mentor decades ago. The older man smiled slightly and nodded, "He undoubtedly knows I am in Ireland. With a man like Blessing, that is enough for him, for now anyway. When will he come for me? I've not decided if he will or won't. Guessing what Mr. Blessing will do, I've learned, is problematic at the best of times."

"You have a plan, doubtless," Clarke said.

"Need you ask? Of course I do. Our little island will make an excellent base of operations. It was once, but was disrupted. That was many years ago. We live in a different world these days though," Manning said.

"To further that end, we need to disrupt the status quo before we can take control. The other, and perhaps most important, part of the plan is to lay hands on the Book and Julian Blessing."

\* \* \*

A dark, heavy feeling lay over Ireland. Storm clouds gathered over the Irish Sea and rushed the craggy coastline. An ominous silence passed over the verdant pasture land ringing the monastery and its prominent chapel.

This had been Julian's home, the sanctuary he was brought to after his return from Rome. It allowed for his physical healing, but the weight of his thoughts held down the spiritual restoration he badly needed.

The remarkably preserved buildings presented a brave face to the storm. The chapel's weathered stones and ancient pillars, with their carved capitals, challenged the weather to do its worst.

But the worst would come from within.

\* \* \*

John Clarke seethed. It was something he was good at. The current focus of his rage was Julian Blessing. "Well, John old boy, this insipid game of Manning's needs to be gingered up a bit. I think some local color would suffice," Clarke said to himself as he stood before the mirror shaving.

* * *

Julian sat in the quiet of the monastery's chapel while the rain fell in sheets outside and a cannonade of thunder rolled in the distance.

His time in New York came to mind. The bitterness of his divorce and the toxic atmosphere of his brokerage house sat heavily on him, but seemed ages ago. A heavy darkness lay on his soul and he always felt sick at heart in those days. Julian found his value as a person was reflected in the price of his clothes or the extent of his portfolio or the car he drove. When he should have been constructing a life he was just building a résumé.

His high octane career on Wall Street initiated him into a world of avarice, duplicity, huge rewards and terrible risks. Still, it presented him a world that never seemed quite real. He spent his time trying not to die and Julian knew there was more to life than that. And he had been right.

His first meeting with Bridget in a park in Lower Manhattan was a eureka moment for him. Meeting her had given him his first glimpse of hope for a meaningful life and a better future than the one he faced alone in New York. She threw him a lifeline when he needed it most. That felt more recent than it was and left him with a warm feeling on a cold night.

He recalled his introduction to Ireland and the village of Cappel Vale. The warm-heartedness of its people was matched only by the rich warmth of the countryside. So many strangers became friends. So many experiences were indelibly engraved on his memory. So many feelings engendered by the people he met and the array of special talents that greeted him.

Moira Hagan had been his teacher. She had introduced him to the mysteries of his new path. Irascible, stubborn and loving, she brought him to a level of understanding that opened his entire world to new possibilities and a life worth living.

The world he knew and the world he would come to know were two very different places. One was a limited reality that enslaved humanity. The other was limitless and liberating, a place where the impossible could and did happen.

Julian's mission to Rome had been a nightmarish cauldron of malignant greed, deceit and death. He immediately became embroiled in a web of treachery that involved money laundering and evil for its own sake.

He had survived, but barely. Others had not been so lucky. Lives destroyed. Lives taken.

His life had become a colorless, featureless landscape as depression took a firm hold on him. A bottomless sadness was matched by an equally deep sense of shame. Then the question had come. Always the same question without an answer. Why?

Why had he been given the talents he had? Why had he been allowed to see both the light and the darkness to straddle the two worlds? Why did his friends die? Why them and not him? Why was it all necessary?

Returning to Ireland had been difficult, but he had nowhere else to go. This was home for him now.

\* \* \*

"When I said we would undermine the current state of Irish affairs, the plan was to take over the republic in an orderly fashion so as not to attract undue attention. Someone blew up a good portion of the Garda Síochána's headquarters today. Not all that subtle would you say?

"You don't know who that someone could be, now do you John?" Manning asked. His voice sounded light, but his face was a mask of rising anger.

"I've not an idea, old boy," Clarke said with a plastic smile. "I've been away taking the country air. I do believe it is advancing our goals though."

"Come now. This stunt has your fingerprints all over it. It is exactly the sort of thing you would do and have done. I'm not saying you did it yourself of course. Too clever for that now, aren't you?" Manning said with a cruel snarl cutting across his face.

"Involving others in our schemes always requires a lot of messy cleanup. I forbid you to pursue this course of action further," Manning said as he slapped his hand on his desk.

Clarke's smile never wavered and his eyes never left Manning's face.

"Your time is coming old man," Clarke said to himself, being sure to keep his thoughts protected. "You are losing it and have outlived your usefulness to me."

\* \* \*

Dr. David Mahoney was a short, older man who cast an impressive presence wherever he went. His face was etched with the lessons that grow wisdom and heartache. Now the man's face was stamped with pain and panic.

"We have a very serious problem," Dr. Mahoney said in a rush, hurrying to Julian's side as he walked the grounds of the monastery.

Julian's look of expectancy furrowed his brow and narrowed his eyes, but he didn't stop walking.

"An Englishman arrived in the village of Chapeltown, just down the road."

"Is that so unusual?" Julian asked.

"The man murdered a local farmer in a pub full of customers and he did it without lifting a finger." The doctor sounded frantic. "And that, by God, is unusual!

"I was in the pub and saw to the victim. The man's chest had been crushed. The Englishman stepped over the body, walked out of the pub and vanished," the doctor said.

Julian's mouth became hard and tight. He stopped and with narrowed eyes, looked out to sea.

"Did you hear me, Julian?" the doctor said with fear animating his voice.

After a moment, Julian said in a voice as cold as the ocean and as hard as the rocks littering the shoreline, "My guess is the mystery Englishman is John Clarke. That would put Manning not too far away." His next words became explosive. "Why is it the innocent always suffer, Doctor? Answer me that."

"Julian," the doctor said. "I'm begging you, have a care. These men are dangerous."

Julian cocked his head at the doctor and smiled a sad smile. "Far more dangerous and deadly than you could possibly know. What you've seen today is only a sample," Julian said. "A very small sample."

\* \* \*

Julian sat brooding before the turf fire in his cottage at the monastery. Ringlets of smoke worked their way up the chimney while wisps escaped to sit at the hearth's edge. A mantle clock set the pace of his disordered thoughts and feelings.

The time was coming. He knew it, could feel it to his core. It wouldn't be long now.

\* \* \*

# CHAPTER TWO

John Clarke admired his reflection in an antique mirror as his mentor harangued him.

"What possessed you to go to that village? I demand an answer," Manning said, as the color continued to rise on his face.

"I was bored with waiting for your time-consuming cat and mouse game to render something in the way of results," Clarke said, while he straightened the knot in his silk school tie. "We are the cat, but Blessing had no idea he was the mouse. Now he does, so carry on with your game. I've just advanced it a bit."

"Tell me you didn't interact with him directly," Manning said.

Clarke thought for a moment. "Directly, no. If I did, he would be dead. Still, he knows about the little incident in the village by now I'm sure."

"That 'little incident' being that you killed a man. Doubtless that was part of your clever plan?" Manning ridiculed.

"Oh no. That was a bonus. Some dirt-clod farmer said something opprobrious to me. Thereupon, he had a heart attack and died. All very sad, but the man forgot his station in life. In the end, it served the plan so it worked out perfectly," Clarke said and smiled into the mirror at the memory of taking a life.

"Just to put my mind at rest that you risked my plans for a worthy cause, what remark did the man make?" Manning asked and his lips twisted into a snarl.

"Something to do with my clothing. Can you imagine it? 'You're looking mighty dapper,' or something to that effect. You know the Irish. Who can understand anything they say? To me, they always sound as if they have a mouth full of soda bread. Oh, sorry, you're Irish aren't you?" Clarke had a mild smile and looked expectant as though praise was about to be laid before him.

"You killed a man who complimented you? Do I understand that correctly? You attracted undue attention out of personal pique? Am I even close to right?" Manning demanded.

"No, actually, I advanced the plan as I said. Some farmer living or dying is of no consequence. The plan is the thing, don't you see? I really don't know why you are belaboring this," Clarke said and produced another bored smile.

"The question you should be asking is 'Do I know where Blessing is?'. In fact, I do know where he is," Clarke said and continued. "Our Mr. Blessing is currently tucked up in an old monastery. Very cozy I should expect."

"First of all," Manning said. "I know and have known right where he is. How do you think I know what you've been up to? The Monastery is where they always go," Manning said.

"You really are a piece of work. If you had done your homework on this, you would know that Blessing will be joined soon by Finbar Clancy. Name ring a bell?"

"Oh, wait. I remember a little something from years ago. Didn't we maim one of his students or something? Wreaked all sorts of havoc if I recall correctly. Talk about pique! The man definitely has no sense of proportion," Clarke said with a smile. "A dwarf isn't he?"

Manning said, "It was many years ago and the student was a far younger and less experienced Bridget Bragonier. Once she recovered, she and that dwarf, as you call him, shut down our entire operation here. Just the two of them, I might add. Walked in on our men and walked out ten minutes later. Do I need to add, few of our men made it out alive and those that did wished they hadn't? You stay away from Clancy. He is the stuff of nightmares," Manning said with force.

"I look forward to making his acquaintance," Clarke said with a broad smile that never reached his gray eyes.

"Well then, I'll start looking for a new protégé right now," Manning said.

He considered destroying his understudy for his insolence, for putting the plan at risk and attracting unwelcome attention. For now, Clarke was useful. How long that would last was a matter of small importance to Terrance Manning.

\* \* \*

"What do you mean you won't be goin'?" said Sean Maher, a huge Irishman with a reputation for bar fights and doing those other things in bars people do in bars. "You said you would go. Oi'm countin' on it."

With her arms crossed over her chest, Julian's teacher, Moira Hagan, stood on the threshold of her cottage in Cappel Vale. She tilted her head back and looked into the eyes of the man who towered over her, over everyone. He broke the gaze first and inspected his shoes.

"Sean Maher, I've not the time to list the things that are oh so very wrong with you. I will simply say you are an eejit." Moira's Irish-accented English was not as broad as Sean's, but hers had the added feature of dripping acid. "I would be thinking that should pretty much cover it, don't you, boyo?"

"But you have to go. What if that unnatural creature, well, does, you know, something unnatural? He is a nasty bit of work that one, Oi can tell you."

Moira let out a noisy breath. "Maher, you are a newly minted member of the Irish Republic's national police force. A force, I'll point out, occasionally as effective as you which is not the compliment it seems," she added as an aside. "Anyway, for this reason, stop your whining. The Gardaí do not whine."

"Next, what would be this something you're talking about? Do you suspect he will make some attempt on your virtue?" she smiled her most licentious smile and winked. "With Finbar Clancy, one never knows." The grin that slashed across her face was of the purest evil.

"Woman, hold your tongue…," Sean stopped before he completed the sentence, but not before he opened the gates of hell.

"What did you say?" the Hagan asked stepping into Maher who backed away instinctively. "Hold your tongue, is that what you were about to say?" Moira spat back cutting Sean off.

"Or what? You forget Maher, you believe I am a witch, but suspect something even darker. I am not a witch of course, but because of your Catholic upbringing, you being an Irishman and a well-rounded eejit, you believe such things.

"So, let's have you be the judge." The woman shot her words through with what could pass for madness. "If I'm a witch as everyone says, I will turn you into a turnip for your insolence. If, however, I am what you and your priests suspect I am, I will make you beg to be turned into a turnip," Moira said.

"Go away, Maher before bad things happen to you. I am not going. Off with ya like a good eejit." She never uncrossed her arms, never moved but the door slammed shut in the sweat-drenched face of Garda Sean Maher. He crossed himself and mumbled, "A witch and a devil is what you are, ya ol' shrew."

The disembodied voice of the Hagan rang out telepathically. "*I heard that, boyo. You'll pay for it later. Now go, get our Mr. Clancy and take him where he needs to go.*" Moira's ghostly voice carried her thoughts. They rang in Sean's head as though she had stormed out of her cottage and shouted them at him.

He quickened his pace and crossed himself again. Once might not be enough. In the case of the Hagan, once was not ever nearly enough.

✳ ✳ ✳

Bridget said into the telephone, "We spoke of it before David so you know, Finbar Clancy will be there later this evening, but as to that other matter…" she paused before continuing, "Julian has mentioned nothing to you of a book?

"I ask because, in a word, that book is dangerous, more so in the wrong hands," she continued. "If my speculation is correct, its contents would ruin everything we've done and push mankind into a new dark age," she whispered. Bridget Bragonier stood straight and graceful, her slim body framed by a window protecting her from the angry weather outside her Dublin home. Iridescent gray eyes looked into a grimy overcast sky.

"No, no mention of a book. But as to Mr. Clancy, I am still concerned, Bridget. Julian's bitterness has ripened even more. I didn't think that was possible. His self-hatred has deepened. It is poisoning him and it will poison others," the doctor said.

"The man who is coming to help Julian is immune to that sort of thing," Bridget said.

"You know him then?" the doctor asked. "He has been here several times, but stays to himself. I can't say I know him."

"He was a teacher of mine. Oh yes, I know him," Bridget said and smiled in fond recollection.

\* \* \*

The Jesuit Book. It was a book that shouldn't exist. There were those who believed it didn't exist. There were those who were afraid to believe it did. There were those who would never stop until they possessed it.

The Book was a repository of secrets, a manual of how to make the unimaginable real and the impossible happen. Its words were strong without the need to be aggressive. They painted images in clear, bright language that brought clarity and a brighter vision of the real world, Julian's world.

He sat alone in the monastery's chapel. Julian reached into his memory. He could feel the Book's leather cover. Each page was a lesson and each lesson was another step toward mastery of his paranormal craft. Written in dozens of languages by scores of different hands, this was not a book one read. It was absorbed, drawn into the core of one's being.

In the early days, and with the help of his teacher, Julian had discovered talents, abilities, powers that shouldn't exist. They did, but not in the reality Julian had known previously. Before he could begin, he had to accept the presence of a truer reality, one that made the impossible entirely possible.

For millennia people walked the path Julian walked now. They were people whose job was to push back the darkness of a hollow reality to help those escape who were trapped within its web of deceit.

These people, these guides existed and exist today on the fringes of two worlds. They know the truth, but see the lie. Two worlds, two realities – one true and one false.

For hundreds of years, there had been members of the Jesuit order who were of the two worlds. They had compiled the Book in secret. Many had protected it at the cost of their lives. Still, others came forward to take their place, to expand the Book and to guard it.

Julian was the Book's protector now. He accepted the Book in Rome and in so doing, took an oath to safeguard it regardless of cost and heedless of the deadly risks.

Julian had absorbed the lessons. He had studied and applied what he learned to his talents. The more he learned, the more talents presented themselves. The more he practiced, the more he learned to trust himself and the more unshakable became his current resolve.

Sometimes the Book's words came to him in his own voice. At other times they were delivered in the harsh whisper of his friend, Father Marek Soski. The priest was a friend Julian felt he helped kill in Rome.

*"Do not try to capture the power,"* the voices of the Book said. *"Do not attempt to hold it as your own. By the time you discover your error in attempting that, you will know you wasted precious time on a task that was never possible.*

*"Let the power, the energy of life move through you. Harness all the energy around you. Channel it from the earth and air, from everything and from nothing. Use every source, past and present, good and bad, wise and foolish that presents itself as it presents itself. Then you will know. This is not about you. It is about the universe."*

For now, the Book was safe.

He closed his eyes and called out softly, "He is here, doctor?" The chapel door opened and Dr. Mahoney entered, his footfalls echoing off the stone floor.

"Do you ever wonder how disconcerting that is?" the doctor asked. "I mean knowing who is on the other side of the door well before you should."

"Are you alarmed, doctor? You don't look especially unsettled," Julian said in a whisper.

"It's with the likes of you I've been dealing for over a dozen years. I've become accustomed to it, but yes, I'm thrown off balance nearly every time. And yes, as you know, he is here."

* * *

Julian and the doctor walked down the corridors of the monastery, the refuge that had been Julian's temporary home.

"What is it you hear when you are out on the cliffs?" the doctor asked. "I've heard it described as echoes, but I've no idea what that means."

Julian answered, "Everyone experiences the echoes differently I guess. You hear them too."

"How so? I'm not one of you, I don't hear any echoes," the doctor said and the look of concentration cut deeply into his forehead.

"But you do. If we quiet our thoughts, we each hear our own echoes. Doubtless, you have had patients who never take their medication and disregard all of your advice. It is as if they don't really want to get better since they are not doing anything to speed their own recovery.

"One of these patients comes to you with a complaint. You know the outcome before you start. You know you can treat the symptoms quickly, easily and safely. But the other choice is to take the longer road and treat the cause of the patient's symptoms. This will be time consuming, difficult and poses some risks and will likely be fruitless," Julian said.

"In cases like these, do you ever have an internal dialogue? 'By treating this patient, in a more comprehensive way' you say to yourself, 'I know I am taking time away from other patients who do want to get better.' By the time that conversation with yourself is over, you know the right thing to do," Julian said. "You've listened to the truer voices' echoes, the ones that push you in the right direction.

"Some echoes, doctor, are easy like that," Julian said. They make sense and they are simple. Others, well, they are nearly impossible to obey, no?" Julian said.

The doctor looked thoughtful as though an inner battle was being fought, a battle of monumental complexity. He took a breath and let his shoulders drop. Julian slumped a little. He smiled a sad smile and looked at and into the doctor.

"Julian," the doctor began. "We've never spoken of it, but are you beginning to find what you came here for?"

"I suppose I came here looking to recuperate, but I've found I needed something else before I can start on any road to recovery. I believe the path leading to that something else begins tonight."

\* \* \*

Sean Maher, glorious in his uniform, shot from the police car. With an outstretched hand and a luminous smile, he rushed at Julian. It was a hand ideal for strangling water buffalo and a smile of indisputable fondness and pleasure.

Julian took the hand and discharged a light electrical jolt that left Sean with tingling fingers and a wary expression.

"Julian, old son." Maher stopped, shocked at what had become of his friend. He tried to cover his alarm and was spectacularly unsuccessful. "It seems like dog years since Oi've set eyes on ya. Ya look fit, boyo." Sean Maher didn't do duplicity well. "Oi see you are up to your old tricks and Oi'll have to punish you when the feeling comes back into me hand."

This was not the Julian he remembered. It was not the man Sean knocked down in a bar in the village of Cappel Vale. It was not the man who had defended the village and rescued a child, fallen in love and saved a witch. He and Julian had been friends since Julian was pulled from his life in New York City to the Irish village near the sea. Sean knew that Julian was there somewhere inside the shell he had created. The big man could feel it and for him, feelings were everything.

"Sean," Julian said. "You are a poor liar. Maybe the worst I've ever met. In fact, you know I look like hell. It is as painful to see me like this as it is for me to be seen," Julian said.

"All that aside, against me better advice, Oi've brought you a visitor." Sean leaned in for a conspiratorial whisper. "Oi will warn you, this is the nastiest piece of work ever wrought by Beelzebub. The creature is a horror and Oi'm warning you to send him away before he can infect you with his evil. He makes the Hagan look like a plaster saint!" Sean said.

"Fortunately, Oi have me faith in God and a good right hand to protect me from both of those two beasts. Coming here it was all Oi could do to keep from giving Clancy the good beating which he deserves altogether. Men or devils don't frighten a Maher," Sean said puffed up with smugness.

"Oi don't think you should be puttin' your soul at such risk as to be capering around with the likes of Finbar Clancy," Sean concluded and jerked his thumb over his shoulder to the waiting patrol car.

"I don't have much of a soul left, so there is little risk there. Doesn't really matter, he is about to frighten the hell out of you," Julian said.

"Ha, frightened is it? Me? You think Oi could be frightened by that troll? Never."

"Sean," Julian said.

"Huh?" the big man asked.

"I hate to mention it, but you'll be screaming like a little girl in just a moment."

\* \* \*

# Chapter Three

Terrance Manning sat in his study and thought dark thoughts. The room's walls were filled with books. It smelled of paper, leather and dust and the fire in the hearth drew threatening visions on the walls.

Clarke had been right in one regard. The plan was the thing and the plan was coming together with individual pieces dropping into place with satisfying snaps.

When would it be completed? He did not know.

How many would need to die in the process? He did not care.

The plan was the thing.

* * *

Sean Maher, a man afraid of few things, chuckled before he screamed, more or less just like a little girl, "Sweet Jasus, Mary and Joseph!" Sean crossed himself and cursed.

Standing entirely too close behind Sean was a small, withered, terminally scruffy man. As he looked up at Maher, the wrinkled man's face appeared to be a little too well acquainted with madness.

His eyebrows seemed to fight his forehead for real estate on an overly large skull. His smile was nothing short of a cruel slash of licentiousness. But his hard gray eyes were at once compelling, terrifying and knowing.

Julian smiled slightly.

"It would be safe to assume you are Julian Blessing. You're the only one mad enough to be seen with this great oaf, Sean Maher. Doubtless, you count him as a friend?"

"I am proud to say he is my friend, yes," Julian answered slowly in a whisper that carried his slight smile.

"Well, more fool you, is all I can say. There is no accounting for taste, I suppose. Tell me, is it your job to protect him? Look at that atrocious lump of quivering shite," Finbar Clancy snorted jerking a thumb in Sean's direction.

Sean swallowed all caution and shot back, "Tempt me not, Finbar," scowling down at the little man.

Clancy doubled over laughing. He caught his breath and wheezed, "Or what, Maher? What is it you think you are going to do? You may frighten others, but not me, boyo. To prove it, step up so I can beat you like I would an old rug. On second thought, being frail and not wanting to over-tire meself, I'll have you beat yourself with your own fists. If you doubt I can, you just give it a go, lad."

Sean's fists were clenched, his eyes screwed shut, his teeth were gritted and he growled. He shook with fury held in check only by the knowledge Finbar Clancy could do everything he said and more. Much, much more.

Clancy turned his attention back to Julian. "Let me ask you a question, young man. What are you looking for?" Finbar asked.

The perennial wind backed off for a moment and the world went silent. Suddenly, Sean lost his taste for murder and shivered at the single word.

Julian's answer was a whisper delivered without hesitation.

"Revenge."

Finbar Clancy looked at the ground and nodded his head. "Right, it seems I've arrived at just the right place at just the right time. Come along. Maher, go home and stick your nose in a pint. If I want anything I'll contact you, otherwise stay away. And keep the rest of your horrible village full of eejits away, too."

\* \* \*

Dr. Mahoney led Julian and Finbar Clancy to a small thatch-roofed cottage Clancy had used before. It sat adjacent to Julian's, both hard by the rocky cliffs. The wind kicked from the Irish Sea and the inky moonless night blocked all but the brightest stars.

One bedroom opened off the main room and a clean, efficient kitchen took up the far wall.

Despite his personal appearance, Finbar Clancy was accustomed to living a tidy, well organized, contemplative life. The interior of his cottage contradicted his fierce-bordering-on-bizarre forest dwelling gnome persona. One wall was covered with bookshelves groaning under the weight of hundreds of volumes. On a Persian carpet of great antiquity sat two sturdy and well-worn rockers placed before a turf fire.

This was a sanctuary within a sanctuary and it was clear this was a house exclusively set up by and for Finbar Clancy.

"I'll just put me things away. Come sit before the fire, Julian, me boy," Finbar called out. "You don't mind if I call you Julian? It doesn't matter since that is what I'll call you regardless," Finbar said.

Julian smiled his slight smile and took a seat near the hearth.

At Finbar's return, both men stared into the fire in a comfortable silence until Finbar spoke.

"Keep in mind, I know a great deal about you but nothing of what you truly want. So, shall I guess or will you be kind enough to tell me?" Finbar asked.

There was no doubt Finbar Clancy was an educated man of advanced years. That he had lived in both worlds for decades was manifestly evident. It would be foolish to try to deceive him. It would be dangerous to cross him.

"All I needed when I returned from Rome was out. Out of this life. Events are conspiring against me though. If you know anything about me, you know it happens a lot. Manning is in the country and will do whatever it takes to draw me out. I am tired of the violence and it has to end, Mr. Clancy," Julian said in a hard whisper.

"Unable to have what I need, what I want now is revenge, for my friends, for me and for all those Manning and Clarke have maimed and killed. Those two must be stopped at any cost. The thought of all that is the only thing that keeps me going. I live and breathe it.

"Without it, there is no way back for me. It ends here and it ends with me." Julian's voice was cold and brittle. "If you can assist me, fine. If not, I need to know that too."

"Now, isn't that always the way of it," Finbar said. "Wants and needs. You would be surprised how many people confuse the two. You would be stunned at how many follow a procession of ultimate silliness – wants become needs become God given rights. All, of course, to be provided by someone else. Rather sad really.

"I will not try to minimize any of your predicament. You are dealing with a soul-shredding set of problems," Finbar began.

"I knew I was dealing with the right sort of person when you used the word revenge. Others would have said justice. That makes the quest sound noble. Life seldom is, Julian.

"You, however, chose a word that gets to the heart of things and strikes a more accurate cord. It is good to see you've not fallen into the common trap of lying to yourself. We can work with that and it is a lot of work we have to do in a short time. So, can I help you? In a word, yes," Finbar said.

"As you say, thoughts of revenge are propelling you forward and doing an exceedingly good job of that. Look at yourself. You're a wreck. If the opportunity for the revenge you seek materialized today, would you be ready to do more than give it a baleful look?" Finbar asked.

Before Julian could answer, Finbar said, "Julian, I will give you a clue. Perhaps it is better to see it as a lifeline. All of what you want, all of what you need, every desire – all of it is possible. The difficult part is, it is up to you to create the methods by which all of it can be yours. Until you do, there will be no moving forward for your fine self."

The old man pulled out a pipe from the pocket of his jacket and began to pack it with tobacco from a leather pouch. The process was slow with well-timed and precise movements. Pinch, pack, pinch, pack, pinch, pack, tamp down, light with a wooden kitchen match, tamp again.

This wasn't about smoking. It was about ritual. It was about taking time to slow down, to think, to consider options, to arrive at a conclusion.

"Sleep on it for the night and we'll talk again in the morning. I'm going to stay up and read 'til my eyes get as tired as you look," Finbar said and took another pull on his pipe. "That may take a while."

# Chapter Four

In the doctor's study at the monastery, Bridget whispered, "Is he any better, David?" Bridget stood erect and elegant, her slim body framed by a window in the doctor's office shielding her from the angry weather outside. "When I spoke with him not long ago, he seemed to be," Bridget said.

"Better is it? Better is a relative word, but useful in this case," the doctor said. "In some ways, yes he is, but in most ways, no. His bitterness has matured, his self-hatred deepened, as I've said. Even with the help of your friend, I fear it will poison Julian. He stands out there for hours. Teetering on the edge seems to give him some slight comfort or punishes him all the more. I've not been able to determine which and he isn't saying.

"As you know, when I brought him to the monastery, he was mute and in the process of closing himself down. He speaks now, but it's little else that's changed. You've talked with him, so you know," the doctor said.

"You can't see any of this?" Dr. Mahoney asked. He sat behind his desk relaxed, astute, professional. A fringe of gray hair set off shrewd, but soft brown eyes. His face wore a concerned expression with his forehead pinched in concentration.

His Irish English was accented like Bridget's. While hers was light, but formal, his was decidedly casual.

Bridget considered a moment then said, "He is gone to me now. He has shut his mind and his heart to me. No, old friend, the second sight will do me no good with him. At least for now."

"That does and doesn't surprise me," the doctor said. "On the one hand, you've seldom failed with your sight. On the other, Julian isn't everyman, now is he." It was a question that wasn't.

"David, I can say only, events are being manipulated so that the future is shrouded. Still, you are right old friend, Julian is not like any other man."

"Bridget," the doctor said. "Over the years, I have had many patients here. Julian is different to be sure, but there is something else. Where others have exercised their talents with vigor as they recovered, Julian is taking a distinctly passive role. It is as though he reacts rather than acts. It seems like he doesn't care. I don't know how to explain it. I don't have the words, but…"

"I understand you completely. To a high degree he has changed. I expected the practice of his talents to change, but in truth I expected him to react in exactly the opposite way to that which you describe. It would not be the first time he has surprised me though," Bridget said. "Where he goes from here is the question.

"I have a question for you, David. Do you think bringing Ailís here now will help?" Bridget asked.

"Help is it? I don't know if it will or won't. There is a risk it might very well hurt the situation."

The doctor said, "People died and I understand some wish they had during his mission in Rome. It transformed him as it would anyone. It is impossible to know if her presence will help or hurt, but nothing ventured, eh?"

Bridget turned to face the doctor as he continued. "Julian told me the entire story. His Dr. Dwyer well might have been killed in Rome. He feels responsible for it all.

"The only way he knows to make amends for the lives taken is to give up his own. He can either do that physically or emotionally, spiritually if you will. It is the same in any case. But I'm not telling you anything you don't know. You told me it happened to your fine self those many years ago, so you know better than anyone," the doctor concluded.

"He is not responsible," Bridget said and there was iron in her voice.

"You are off your game, my dear. It isn't like you to state the obvious. Still it isn't what we know or even believe. It is what he believes that matters. It is his truth that has meaning.

"He will continue to punish himself until he is lost to us altogether or finds himself. Either process will be painful. That is, unless he can be stopped and that won't be easy." The doctor took off his wire rimmed glasses, knuckled his eyes and said, "He is not a man easily swayed. Back to the other question though.

"Dr. Ailís Dwyer. Now there is a remarkable woman to be sure. I knew her before, you know. She and I worked in the same hospital. She was a lowly resident while my august self was, well, august." The man chuckled. "She was hard headed and brilliant then. She is more so now. She won't be easily fobbed off. She will want a diagnosis and my assessment. Sad it is, but I have little to give.

"Bridget, you brought her here, but before she leaves she will want answers from me. What am I allowed to tell her?"

"After she returned with him from Rome, Ailís stayed with me. We talked. She knows. At least she knows as much as she is willing to accept. What she knows more than anything is that she loves him and will give up her own life to save his." Bridget's sigh was empty and her angular face and gray eyes reflected the pain she felt for them all.

"As a prognosis goes, mine will do little good," the doctor said.

"Tell her what you know, David." Bridget paused and changed the line of the discussion with a question. "When did he begin talking to you?"

"A fortnight ago, no more. I wouldn't let him speak telepathically. I made him say the words or keep his thoughts to himself. He needed me to agree with him, to see him as he sees himself and to condemn him. By the time he found out I wouldn't convict him of crimes he did not commit, it was too late to lapse back into silence."

"Well played, David," Bridget said and smiled slightly.

"I thought so, but it is very few I've played well with Julian. His mind is knife-edge sharp. He hides his talents from me but experience says they are beyond my ability to calculate. I can tell you, his mental discipline is nearly unreasonable. He is seldom not fully on his game," the doctor said.

"No, he doesn't let me get away with much and I'll tell you, the effort is wearing me out. I've never had a case like this and hope to never have another." The doctor picked up his glasses and rested them on the tip of his nose.

"Bridget, an odd thing happened. My patients all crave the absolute solitude of this place. I thought Julian would be the same in spades. He had a package when he arrived, perhaps the book you mentioned. A man came to see Julian. They spent some time together. The man took the package away," the doctor said. The ease with which he said it was something he did not feel. "Something just seemed strange about Julian and his visitor."

"Who the visitor is, I do not know. I am sure the package would be the book he had when he returned from Rome. That book is a disturbing piece of the puzzle. In any case, he has the money to assure its safety, so we won't be getting at it any time soon. As to the identity of his visitor, Julian has shielded it from me," Bridget said and turned back to the window.

She watched Ailís approach Julian from behind and step up beside him. A moment passed and Julian turned.

✻ ✻ ✻

Standing next to him, Ailís Dwyer said, "Shall we? Jump I mean. We need only step off the edge." She peered over the cliff. "Mind you, the rocks will make a terrible mess of us."

Julian turned. His thought was a whisper as soft as Ailís' chestnut hair and filled with longing for a time he knew had past. He looked into her hazel eyes and thought, *I have missed feeling you near me.* Each word was slow and deliberate.

She felt his thought and answered, "And where is it you've missed me, Julian? Here?" she said and slid her hands from his shoulders to his wrists. "Or here?" she asked placing her hand over his heart. "Or is it only here?" she touched her fingers to his temple.

She took Julian by the arm. Her hand slid into his and she walked him to his cottage on the monastery grounds, near the headlands.

\* \* \*

Dr. Mahoney canted his head to the side and said, "You'll be staying the night? You and Dr. Dwyer? 'Tis a long drive back to either Dublin or the village."

"No," Bridget said. "I will be returning to the village. I am to meet Moira there. I feel sure Ailís and Julian have much to discuss. That is my hope in any case. Moira and I will return to fetch our Ailís tomorrow. With luck, we will be bringing Julian home also."

\* \* \*

The cottage was lit solely by the turf fire. Shadows emerged on the walls, entwined and danced slowly away as Ailís took Julian to a rocking chair facing the hearth. She took his face in her hands and lightly brushed her lips against his. She felt him take in a breath and hold it, then heard him moan as the need for her built inside him.

"You are cold as ice. As your doctor, I'm ordering you to go take a hot shower. And you're to stay there until you are warm from the inside out," Ailís said playfully.

Again, she took his face in her hands and saw the loneliness and longing in his eyes. "Go, my love. Take your shower. Afterwards we can talk if you want. Or not. It all depends on you."

Julian nodded once and rose from his chair slowly, painfully.

Ailís began to unbutton his shirt. "I can do that," Julian said in a strained whisper.

"I know you can, but I enjoy helping," Ailís said and smiled up at him.

With great care she manipulated each shirt button, then undid the buttons at his cuffs. Her arms encircled his body and she felt how slight he had become. She laid her head on his chest and heard a strong heartbeat and even breaths.

"Off with you. Into the shower. Just let the hot water beat on you for a while. You'll feel better when you're warm. Are you hungry?" Ailís asked.

Julian tried to smile and shook his head before heading off.

"Shave while you're at it," she called after him and he could hear the smile in her voice.

\* \* \*

As instructed, Julian let the scalding water drum against his skin. He felt the water land on his shoulders and chest and roll down his body. He smiled. She had been right. She usually was. The water seared his skin and warmed him, allowing his muscles to relax a little and to forget a little.

Steam built up in the bathroom and each breath of warm, moist air seemed to restore him. He slowly shaved in the shower. He felt good to have his face clean shaven again.

After what Ailís thought was an inordinately long time, Julian emerged from the bathroom in a cloud of steam. He had a towel around his waist and one over his shoulders. He approached the bed where Ailís was tucked up under the covers.

"Ailís," he said and shook his head sadly. "You don't understand. I can't. I don't. There are no words to explain what is happening to me."

"Come to bed, my love," Ailís said. After a moment, his towels dropped to the floor and he slid under the sheet.

Ailís ached. It felt like ages since she had been touched. It felt as if she couldn't get close enough to him as she strained against his body.

His hands were as she remembered. Warm and tender, his touch on her bare skin sent a burst of heat straight to her center.

"Love, when we came in here tonight we left the world outside. This night is about us and for us." She put her lips to his and found them warm and inviting.

A small sound escaped from her lips as she kissed his neck and began to explore his body with her mouth.

Julian needed to feel her warm skin, feel her strong body against his. He needed to know there was a possibility of a normal life outside the two worlds. His fingers stroked her hair and her skin, so soft and silky to the touch.

He needed to feel the curve of her waist, the arch of her back. He needed to feel the delicious torment of wanting her as he had wanted her when they first met.

He pulled her to him and covered her mouth with his. They each groaned as her skin heated to his touch.

Thunder echoed outside and rain began to beat gently on the thatched roof.

Julian captured her mouth and she felt the same need he had for her. She stopped, pulled back, swept back in and brushed his lips with hers. His hands gathered her face and pulled it to him, his fingers intertwining in her luxurious hair.

Fire and passion ignited as his tongue dove between her lips. He tasted her, felt her, pulled her to him. He needed and wanted her. Her tongue coiled around his. Julian crushed her mouth to his as her supple fingers slid into his hair to pull his mouth against hers.

Ailís lost herself, gave herself to him willingly and completely and he to her. This was a world for just the two of them.

* * *

The early morning air had its usual wintertime bite. Ailís pulled her coat tightly around herself as she and Julian stood on the cliff's edge. The salt spray intensified the cold. She wasn't cold, she was numb.

"Are you gone from me, Julian?" she asked in a whisper drenched in agony. "Let me say only, no matter how you think you have changed, my feelings for you have not and will not." She watched as the man she loved lowered his head, closed his eyes and exhaled.

He was lost to her. He was lost to them all. Mostly, he was lost to himself.

Julian would have wept, but he had no tears left.

* * *

Bridget stood in Dr. Mahoney's office. She slumped slightly as she watched Ailís turn and walk slowly back toward the doctor's office. Bridget shifted her attention and found Julian looking at her. Given the distance, she knew he couldn't see her, but she knew he did. He had become too good not to.

*"You should not have brought her here, Bridget. It was unfair and unkind regardless of your intent,"* Julian transmitted his thought. *"I do not deserve her and she does not deserve what I have become."*

Bridget felt Julian's thought more powerfully than any she had ever experienced from anyone. The words came to her slowly, with deliberation and precision.

*"As I said before, you are changed in some ways certainly, but at base you are still the same. Julian, you are the man she loves."* Bridget paused. *"I see you have chosen to make decisions for Ailís though. That's new, is it not?"* She left the thought there.

*"We make choices every day,"* Julian countered. *"Some are of little consequence. Others we pay for every day for the rest of our lives. Judging by the havoc I have left in my wake, which kind of choices do you suppose I have made recently?"* Julian turned into the wind and the Irish Sea.

*"You assume too much, Julian,"* she said.

*"Bridget, I assume it all. Every choice I made that led to every death – I assume responsibility for them all."* The wind backed and he staggered but maintained his position and posture.

*"That is not what I meant,"* she thought and received his answer immediately.

*"I know, but it was what I wanted you to hear from me."* His thought was clear and his resolve irrevocable. He had set himself adrift as he floated in a sea of anguish. He was gone from them. For now.

\* \* \*

Bridget drove while Ailís sat in silence on the return trip to the village of Cappel Vale. It was the location of her home, her son, her practice and patients, and her friends. There was a time she would have said, 'her life and her love,' but her love was standing on a lonely precipice hard against the Irish Sea and her life was in shambles.

Moira Hagan, Julian's teacher, sat in the back seat of the car in a dark silence. She had, at Bridget's suggestion, accompanied them to the monastery. Moira had stayed with the vehicle as Bridget met with Dr. Mahoney and Ailís went to Julian. The notion of the place did not sit well with Moira. Hers was a rural life filled with complex problems and simple solutions.

"Too much brooding," the Hagan said. "And not enough takin' a stick to the problem." It was always difficult to tell if she meant that metaphorically. Probably not, given her history.

"It is my fault, you know," Ailís whispered.

The tires of the car laid down a bit of themselves as the brakes ground the vehicle to a stop. A fishtail or two and Bridget had maneuvered the car to the side of the road. She nonchalantly ignored the honking of other drivers.

"Moira," Bridget said, "I really wish you would not do that. Simply ask me to stop the car and I shall."

Moira Hagan ignored her friend. Although once refined and cultured herself, Moira Hagan had been forced by a hard life to take on the ways of rural Ireland. Her gray eyes were penetrating and her voice acidic at times. This was such a time.

"For the love of whatever god you believe in. Are there any other disasters you want to take responsibility for? How about the Troubles or the Potato Famine?

"Listen well, my fine colleen, if 'tis no help you want to be, well, by all means continue as you are. If, however, you want to be of some small assistance, give over with this 'poor, sad, heartbroken me' business," Moira scoffed. "We have a job of work to do."

"Moira, thank you," Bridget said pleasantly as she glared into the rear view mirror.

"Then you handle her. The girl tries my patience." Moira sat back in the seat and scowled a nearly audible scowl.

"Tell me Ailís, for what are you responsible? You have touched on this before, but you have not said the words until now. Responsible for what, my dear?" Bridget asked and then waited. She was prepared to sit by the side of the road forever if that was necessary.

Minutes passed before Ailís' tear choked voice broke the silence. "Had I not gone to Rome, none of this would have happened. He would have gone about his business and been safely home by now. I was his Achilles heel, the one chink in his armor they could exploit. Everything that happened, happened because I was selfish and wanted to be with him." She covered her face with her hands and wept in shoulder-shaking sobs.

Bridget didn't need to look in the mirror, but she did. She watched Moira soften and let out a noisy breath.

*"I see no recourse but to cut off all avenues that will lead to further recrimination,"* Bridget thought and Moira felt. *"She is crippling herself and eventually will undermine others,"* Bridget continued.

*"She is suffering, but I see no other way than to take a strong hand with her. She is iron willed and would shake off anything less."*

Moira looked back at Bridget in the mirror, considered for a moment and nodded her head once.

Bridget weighed her options. Her voice lost its sweet, lyrical quality and took on the hard edge of a scythe. A very sharp scythe. "Ailís." Bridget turned to face the doctor. "I cannot deliver you to Cappel Vale in this condition and with these thoughts in your mind. We will handle this here and now and we will not speak of it again.

"The things at stake in Rome were far larger than any of us knew. Julian was there because he was supposed to be there. He was the best person for the job even though none of us, including him, knew what the job was.

"Believe me, my dear, your part in all of this was at most, insignificant, so do not believe you were all that important in the vast scheme of things."

Bridget continued her creeping barrage. "You have a job to do, several actually. We all do. You, doctor, are going to return to your village and your son and your patients and you are going to carry on. It is your job to reassure the villagers. Julian is taking some time away and nothing more. He is doing fine and will be back before long. Although we are heartsick over this, there is no reason everyone has to be.

"Ailís, do you understand? It is important that you do. I require an answer and will accept it now." Bridget's gray eyes were piercing, unyielding. She had left no room to maneuver. "Do. You. Understand," Bridget said again. It was not a question, but an order.

Ailís wanted kind words and understanding from her friends. She was not prepared for the ferocity of what she was hearing. Her hands were closed into tight fists and she bit down hard on her lip. She nodded once.

Bridget took two calming breaths and said softly, "We all have our parts to play. Julian has been through a great deal. He will emerge from this changed to be sure and changed in ways we cannot foresee.

"Our goal now is to bring him back in whatever form we can. There is much work he needs to do and he needs to be ready to do it. You may trust, more is at stake than you know," Bridget said.

"Ailís, it is important for you to take care of you and yours. Your strength and your resilience will be vital if we are to bring him back. You must be ready to play your part, as I have said. You must be ready for his return." Bridget turned back in her seat and placed her shaking hands on the steering wheel.

She looked into the rear view mirror again. Moira had a smug twist to her mouth and an arched eyebrow. *Remind me of this when I think to cross you,* Moira thought and Bridget suppressed a smile.

The whisper that broke into their thoughts came from Ailís. "And what if he never returns? What if he can't or won't?"

The voice that floated from the back seat was strong and assured. It brooked no argument and allowed no leeway, but was not unkind. "It is a great deal of time I spent with our Mr. Julian Blessing. You may trust, lass, he is not so easily got rid of. I know. I gave it my best."

\* \* \*

# CHAPTER FIVE

"Can you hear them Julian?" Finbar Clancy asked. "The echoes, I mean. Can you hear them out there on the cliffs more clearly then say in…"

Julian interrupted the older man's question. "Out there, it is easier to concentrate, to feel. At least as far as I feel anything anymore," Julian said. "As for the echoes, probably, but they can come to me anywhere. You know all of that though."

Finbar asked, "You and me and those like us, we all hear the echoes, but hear them differently. What is it you hear?"

"I don't know about others. I hear the past. In the beginning, I heard and saw a time long, long past. Sometimes it was a time as far back as before the world changed. Had it not changed, you would be out of work. I'm sure that is a thought that brings you great comfort," Julian said, but the sarcasm rolled off his companion.

"That was then," Julian continued. "Now, I hear echoes of the recent past, but it is restricted. I hear and see my friends die over and over again. They stand out. They are stark against the mist that clouds us all.

"When I want a respite from the weather I take refuge in the chapel. They follow. They are always with me, Finbar. They stand in silent accusation. They haunt me waking and sleeping, surrounding me always and everywhere. Not much you can do to fix that I suppose," Julian said with a sad frown creasing the corners of his eyes.

* * *

"Finbar, tell me about Ireland. What makes it a special place for those like us? The echoes are stronger here. I hear them more clearly, feel them more intensely then I did in Rome or New York," Julian said. That much I know, but why are people drawn here? Why is Manning here? What does he want that Ireland has?"

"Well, since you ask, I'll start this way. I will agree with you, Ireland is a special place. For the first part of your question, the why of it is easy enough.

"Since the early times, the Celtic people have had to develop two very different turns of mind. They seem incompatible, but listen to me story.

"On the one hand we have built up a tough minded pragmatism," he explained. "We deal with the world as we find it. No theories or speculations, just hard headed realism. When you've been in-vaded as many times as we have, it is best not to have too rosy an outlook.

"At the same time, we know there is more. Our ancient religions taught us the wonder and whimsy, yes whimsy, of everyday things and thus of everyday life.

"As a people and a place, we are ideally suited to dealing with the dark and the light. By nature, we are built to see each and tell the difference between the two.

"For this reason, many of us are called to this place. Could you practice so easily where you came from? The answer is probably no. There are too many distractions and too little belief in what might be possible if we allow ourselves to truly see," Finbar concluded and looked thoughtfully over his pipe at Julian.

"And Manning?" Julian asked.

"For all the reasons I pointed out, he is looking for a base of operations, of course, and this place is nothing short of ideal for his purposes," the old man said. "And what he will do with our island is nothing short of pure devastation, enslavement and evil," Finbar said.

The men walked without particular purpose or haste, but in silence, toward an uncharted future.

* * *

Moira Hagan had the mayor of Cappel Vale by the throat. Literally.

"I don't need to do this physically, but I wanted to get up to my elbows in your vitals," she hissed as Mayor Cahill squirmed.

In the last month the village began to look like someone had turned a Renaissance festival upside down and given it a shake.

"I gave you an assignment a cabbage could carry out flawlessly. You, being an eejit, did not get it right. 'Put an advert in a newspaper in America telling of our part of the world,' I said. You put it in the most-read paper on earth and explained we were a Mecca for witches, aye and all types of new age fools as well. Greater fools than you, if that can be believed," Moira seethed.

"And what are you doing? You are selling maps to 'the sacred spots', if rumor can be trusted. And it can. Fortunately for you, there have been so many visitors they have spilled over into the surrounding countryside, and the locals can make some money off your stupidity," Moira said.

"Every farmhouse and sod hut has been turned into something called a bed and breakfast to fleece the visiting sheep," Moira said.

"If that wasn't enough, should our visitors grease your nasty palm, you will let them in on some filthy lie you make up on the spot," Moira concluded.

"And what sort of lies are they? Druids, aye and real witches. You'll point 'em out for a price. I heard tell, you put one set of witches onto another set of witches and caused no end of dismay. It ended in tears of course," Moira said.

"That's not true," the mayor gasped. "The maps yes, but not the druids and witches part. On me mother's grave."

"Keep your lies to yourself and leave your mother out of this. Listen sharp, little man. We are up to our trotters in witches and I want the herd greatly thinned. It is up to you to do just that. Now get to it before I become unpleasant," Moira snarled.

The mayor scampered away in abject terror. He was a mayor in need of a good plan and a drink. A better plan this time than his last good plan, but any drink would do.

* * *

Finbar knew Julian was a potent force. Others had said as much and the old man had felt it.

What he wasn't prepared for was Julian's mastery or his intensity. He gave himself no quarter. An exercise went perfectly or it was repeated until it did. He would work for hours, far past Finbar's ability to keep up.

The practice made him stronger, but the discussions Julian had with Finbar only opened room for doubt and doubt was something of which Julian already had a surplus.

He said one morning, "Finbar, you say redemption and revenge are incompatible. You've hinted but not said it outright that revenge isn't an option for those of us who occupy the two worlds. Yet aren't we in the retaliation business? Don't we face off daily with false reality and those who perpetrate it? Isn't it our job to stop them? If that is the case, isn't it sometimes necessary to find redemption while seeking justice?" Julian whispered his question.

Finbar Clancy drew on his pipe, smiled and said, "Well, there is no doubt you are every bit the bright little spark everyone says you are.

"You ask the only question worth asking. In fact, I can't answer your question because I don't know the answer. That is, I don't know your answer and that's the way of it. There are questions we each must answer for ourselves," Finbar said. "This is such a one."

"Julian, the path each of us walks is a lonely one. What we have in common is that each of us discovered our individual answers on our own. No one can give you your answers, as no one can give you your talents. It is for you to do and find alone. I'll wager even your book didn't hold all your answers."

"But here I am babbling about what you know too well," Finbar said. "Go about your exercises and discover your own truths."

* * *

Finbar went still and held up his hand to Julian as they practiced in an open pasture away from the monetary.

"Lad, listen sharp. I want to knock you down a few times. Nothing painful, just do as I say." The little man dispatched a charge of energy that caught Julian in the center of the chest. He staggered then fell.

"I thought you said nothing painful. That hurt like hell," Julian said.

"You're too trusting," Finbar laughed. "Now get up so I can do it a few more times. Remember, don't defend yourself. We are play acting for an audience of one. One we can't afford to trust."

Julian nodded his agreement and was dutifully knocked down half a dozen times. Each hit engendered more creative swearing than the last.

Again, Finbar held up his hand. "Did you sense it? Of course you did. It was daft of me to ask."

"I did. Why don't we sit for a while?" Julian asked.

"Now why do you suppose someone would be watching the two of us?" Finbar asked.

"Must you always ask questions to which you already know the answers?" Julian asked.

"Must you always answer questions with questions?" Finbar asked. Both men smiled, but the smiles melted as the glint could be seen from a pair of binoculars in the distance.

It was too far to tell who was behind those glasses, but both men knew and the knowledge saddened them.

\* \* \*

"Is it bad, do you suppose, Taoiseach\*? Is there no way out?" his assistant, Edward Brennen asked.

The Taoiseach, the prime minister of the Irish Republic, rubbed his chin with the back of his hand, looked down onto Dublin's Merrion Street and thought.

Donald Connelly was a man of 70 years or so, of medium height and medium weight. In every way he was medium. He was everyman to everyone. Three things set him apart from thousands of other politicians. He was powerful beyond words, he was cunning beyond the ability to measure and he was Taoiseach.

"Yes, it is very bad and I do not suppose it, lad. I know it as a fact. I honestly don't know how it could be worse," Connelly said and a vicious scowl cut across his face. "You know it as well as I do. A letter bomb exploded at Gardaí headquarters. A few more were intercepted before they reached their intended victims.

"I can get away with saying it was a gas leak, but I'll not be able to do that more than once and trust me lad, there will be more bombings. Much more of this and the people will become restless and that is always bad," Connelly said.

"To make it worse, this comes when one of the cabinet ministers is leaking information to the press. Oh yes, one of my colleagues has taken it upon himself to poison the public against me and so turn the tide in Parliament. I fear we shan't know who the bomber or the quisling is until it is far too late," Connelly said and pounded his right fist into his left palm in frustration.

"Is there something we can do to discover the source of either or both of these? You must have resources. You always do, Taoiseach," Brennen pressed his boss.

Connelly's eyes narrowed and he smiled a cheerless smile. "There is one resource I can call down. Believe me, boyo, I wouldn't do it if it could be avoided, but there are no choices." The man thought for a moment, pinching the bridge of his nose. "I have nothing on her, no one does, no one dares. I'll need to apply pressure another way to gain some advantage I can bargain with.

"I need you to go see someone, a woman here in Dublin," Connelly said.

"Taoiseach, I believe a better choice of messenger is young Thomas," Brennen said with a smile.

"As you say then. Please send our Mr. Ahern. He will have his task cut out for him. Alas, we all have our work to do," Connelly said. "And better Thomas than you, eh? Lad, you'll make a splendid politician."

{*Taoiseach, pronounced: Tea-Shaw}

\* \* \*

The fashionably dressed young man sat in his car on a biting cold night. It was 4:07 A.M. The store had been closed since eleven o'clock. The last of the employees had locked up and left at midnight.

The explosion blew out the four sets of plate glass windows, spewing glass and metal across the road and into the River Liffey.

The pipe bomb placed in the refrigerator section of Supervalu grocery store on Aston Quay didn't have to be overly powerful. Everything around it had the potential to turn into shrapnel with very little incentive. The young man only needed to place his device in the right location.

Had the explosion taken place at 4:07 P.M., the busiest time for the store, the casualty toll would have been horrendous and injuries horrific.

At the headquarters of An Garda Síochána, the message was clear. The timing wasn't a mistake.

Message received.

*** 

"This is an outrage!" Professor Reginald Bragonier said to his wife, Bridget, the fury plain on his face as his eyes flashed and his color rose.

The professor was a small, intense, unfailingly rumpled man. British by birth and education, he found himself a professor of history at Trinity College, Dublin. This was an irony lost on no one but him.

"My darling," Bridget said smoothly. "An outrage would be an Englishman teaching history to the Irish. What is it you find so distracting now?" She smiled as she goaded him.

"The university has put me on notice that my position is to be eliminated," he said in anger and frustration. "Me! Made redundant! I've been wedded to that institution for thirty-five years. It is an outrage, I tell you!"

Bridget's eyes narrowed in concentration and concern, but she said, "Reginald, you have been wedded to me for thirty-five years. It is nearly forty with the university. A detail, but let us not forget it."

Her forehead creased in thought, her eyes narrowed further as she said, "Tell me, from where does this edict come?"

"It was delivered on the quiet by the university president, but he let me know legislation is being drafted to install only native Irish speakers to hold teaching positions," the professor harrumphed and fell heavily into a Queen Ann chair.

"Well, we will have to wait and see what happens, won't we?" Bridget was thoughtful, but a smile crept quietly to her lips. She could see something of the future and had formed something of a plan.

"That's it? Wait and see? Really? That is your best advice?" A vein distended at his temple.

"I suppose we could storm the government buildings with a list of demands," Bridget said. "I am busy this week, but we could do it Tuesday next. Would that do?" Bridget asked with mischief in her eyes.

"This is serious business and you are intentionally provoking me." The professor leaned forward in his chair trying to make his cherubic face look threatening.

"Of course I am, my dear. It is one of the little pleasures I derive from life. I live for these opportunities." Bridget turned thoughtful. "Still, there is nothing but to wait and see. I think we will not have long to wait and we certainly will see. Do not ask me how I know, but this has more to do with me than you."

A hall clock set a metronome's precision to the distracted silence that enveloped them.

* * *

The village of Cappel Vale was a simple affair. It had grown of late, but the residents would never allow progress to interfere with the way their village had been for a hundred years.

The main thoroughfare started at the police station and continued to St. Michael's Catholic Church. In between those book ends were a collection of merchants, medicaments, light machinery repair, pubs and a doctor. In short, everything anyone could ever want providing you never lived outside of Cappel Vale.

After passing through the business section of the village, one was stunned by the riot of flowering plants and shrubs. The houses had a sameness but each offset that with brightly painted doors and shutters and gardens that could win awards.

Just out of the shadow of the church was Moira Hagan's cottage. The front yard was crowded with plants of every kind in lush abundance and all seeking space. Tea roses fought with thyme and garlic, rosemary and peppermint and the Hagan looked on with a benign eye.

"We're looking for the way," a thirty-something witch with a bad haircut said.

Moira was working in her garden and assumed anyone who would ask such a question, and ask it of her, was mentally unhinged. Best not to encourage such folk, she thought.

"A blessing on you, madam, but we are looking for the way," the witch said again.

Moira stopped what she was doing and turned to find thirteen men and women between the ages of twenty and seventy standing at her garden gate. Some were professionals in their day-to-day lives, some students, some retired, some in between. Moira could sense them all with ease. They were believers willing to trust enthusiastically. Each possessed only enough guile to fool themselves.

Long robes were covered by longer hooded cloaks. Some were of rich brocade while others were rough wool. Some were unadorned while others were festooned with Celtic symbols and amulets. Others still were decorated with complex looking faux runes. Some were obviously custom made while some were homespun witch uniforms.

Although different in nearly all ways, two things uniformly animated these people – faith and a sincere desire to be part of something unique, important and bigger than themselves.

"The way to where?" Moira asked and instantly regretted it.

"Uh, enlightenment? Unity with the universe?" the lead witch asked with the simplicity of a child.

"Well, you stopped at the wrong door today. I'm not in the enlightenment business. Now go away before I become unhappy," Moira said and returned to her gardening.

"Yeahbut, you are a witch. Everyone says so. Well, except the mayor who wanted us to tell you he said you are totally not a witch," the witch said.

"Everyone is wrong except the mayor. That isn't the usual way, but it happens sometimes. Now, go away." Moira was emphatic.

"Yeahbut, being a witch, you have an obligation to teach others the way."

"You have been vastly misinformed Miss Yeahbut. I am not a witch. I do not have to teach anyone. I don't know about the way you are referring to and I am under no obligation to anyone for anything. And never have been," Moira said and the steam began to build.

"You! Miss Yeahbut, do you have a name?" Moira demanded.

"Who me?" the witch leader asked. She motioned her coven to remain while she approached Moira alone. Some would later say this was bravery. Others would hint at lunacy. "I'm Lavonia Grayhawk."

"Now you are an eejit and a liar. What is your real name and be quick about it," Moira said.

"Bobbi Ann Shultlitzen, but I prefer Lavonia Grayhawk," Lavonia said.

"I don't doubt that you do prefer it. So be it, Miss Grayhawk. Listen sharp. I never repeat myself, but I will this once because you are Americans and thus not all that bright." Moira continued with force and took a step toward the assembled witches-in-training. "Go. Away."

Lavonia and her witches retreated to what they thought was a safe distance. They were wrong. Wrong was getting to be a habit with them.

"Well, even though you are unkind, a blessing on you, madam," Lavonia said and bowed her hasty farewell, wobbling off in a huff with her fellow witches in tow.

* * *

Ailís' home and her practice were in the same building. Examination rooms and a compact surgical suite took up the front of the house's first floor. The original sitting room served as a comfortable waiting area for patients.

A large kitchen and dining room took up the remainder of the back of the house with bedrooms on the second floor.

"Mama," Timothy said. "Everyone keeps asking me if Mr. Julian will be back soon. I think they are afraid to ask you or Mrs. Hagan. What should I tell them? Why doesn't he just come home?"

Dr. Ailís Dwyer stopped cutting vegetables for their dinner, walked to the kitchen table and pulled out two chairs. She took one and invited her son to join her.

She looked into the soft eyes of her son and saw there the concern and the confusion she felt herself. The boy was nearly twelve years old he was proud to point out, small for his age, bright and quick. She knew her son as only a mother could and knew only the truth would satisfy him. She couldn't offer the whole truth, but she could be economical with it.

"Timothy, let's handle this in two parts. Mr. Julian was hurt while he and I were in Rome. He is taking time to rest and to recover his strength. He felt he could do that easier and faster away from here. You know how he is. He would never want to be a worry or a burden.

"Between you and me, I think he was a wee bit embarrassed to have people see him as he is. He wants to return whole and happy, the way he left." Her eyes clouded for a moment. It was a moment Timothy noted but dismissed not knowing the cause.

"Well, makes sense that does. When he took that beatin' a year ago, he looked awful. Is it that bad again?" the boy asked.

"That is the second part. I will tell you the truth, Timothy, although it must go no further than you and me. Not all of his injuries are the kind you can see, but they are there and they are painful none the less," she said.

"Sometimes the deepest scars are the ones you don't see." She wanted to reassure her son, but she believed none of the reassurances she gave. "You can ask Mrs. Hagan. She says he will be back soon.

"Mr. Julian will tuck up and he'll be good as new before long. In the meantime, he just wants to avoid people and we're to help him do that."

His brow wrinkled in concentration, Timothy said, "Why not just come back home, come back to Cappel Vale? The village would make him welcome. Ach, you and me would make him welcome, I know."

"Enough of this. He has his reasons and I have mine for telling you to go wash up for supper. Off with ya," the doctor said.

Timothy jumped up, kissed his mother's cheek and ran off. Ailís slumped in her chair and blinked back the tears that brimmed her eyes. "I don't care if he is good as new. I just want him back," she whispered.

* * *

"Oh, I feel slighted, Mr. Ahern," Bridget said with a mock pout. "I cleaned up the parlor and dressed especially nicely to greet the Taoiseach. His offices are not far from here, so it could not be the distance that kept him away. No, it must be something about me. I am crushed, I tell you." Bridget smiled slightly.

The prime minister's aide couldn't stop his hands from shaking. His mouth was dry and he needed a drink. He could feel the immense personal power that emanated from his hostess. Her intellect was frighteningly sharp. All the while, she controlled everything about this interview with impeccable manners and grace, and a veiled edge that threatened to fillet him at any moment. He had no doubt she would do it with a smile.

He cursed his boss for the hundredth time for throwing him under the tram that was Mrs. Bridget Bragonier.

"The Taoiseach is filled with nothing but regret that he is unable to meet with you personally, Mrs. Bragonier."

With plate glass smoothness Bridget cut in. "Is that what he is filled with? I have always wondered." She smiled and tilted her head.

The young man swallowed hard and continued. "It is affairs of state that have called him away. You may believe nothing less would have kept him from visiting with you."

"Well," Bridget said, "nothing that is, but the purest fear. You may leave the artifice if you would not mind. It seems to make you nervous and that will not do. While you are my guest, it is my responsibility to make you comfortable." Sweetness dripped from her voice. "What is it you want of me, young man?"

Bridget looked at and into the man. For his part, Ahern's smile turned pathetic, but he relaxed some and collapsed inside some more.

They were seated in Bridget's front room. It was a spacious refuge of soft, shimmering white set off with dark mahogany occasional tables and Waterford crystal lamps.

"Madam." The young man drew a breath. "Thank you for your kindness. The Taoiseach finds himself in a difficult predicament. He is faced by two staggering catastrophes.

"State secrets are being leaked by, it is believed, a member of his cabinet. We must find the leak before any more damage can be done to the Republic and the Irish people." He drew a breath. "There is also another matter," Ahern said.

"Someone, as yet to be determined, posted a letter bomb to the police last week which detonated. No one was killed in that attack. Just yesterday another bomb was intercepted addressed to the Archbishop of Dublin."

"Still, the question remains, what is it Mr. Connelly wants from me?" She looked expectant.

"Uh, Mrs. Bragonier, it is the belief of the Taoiseach you have, um, a special, uh, talent when it comes to, well, divining the true thoughts of others and seeing into the future," he finished in a rush.

Bridget gave a light chuckle. "So he believes I am the Delphic oracle? How very interesting. Please, continue with the rest of your master's message."

The young man began to hyperventilate and perspiration stood out on his forehead. "Please, Mrs. Bragonier," he bleated.

"The rest of the message, if you please." Her tone was flat and her smile did nothing to soften her eyes.

He swallowed hard again. "The Taoiseach authorizes me to say pending legislation that would impact the teaching staff at our universities could be made to disappear if, please Mrs. Bragonier, don't make me do this."

"I wish to clarify something. I am elderly, as you can see, and so when it comes to murky business I am often times in need of clarification."

The young man nodded and knew two things. First, nothing in her last sentence was true and second, this was about to turn even more unpleasant. Again he cursed his boss.

"To get at the heart of the matter, if I am willing to help the Taoiseach with his current difficulties, he will remove the sword he is dangling over my husband's head? More tea?"

The man could only make strangled noises and nod and shake his head alternately.

"Young man, since we seem to be bartering as though we were at some country horse fair, I will make you an offer. I will take away your suffering by ending this charade if you will repeat my words verbatim to the Taoiseach."

The man was eager and vigorously nodded his head in agreement. He searched his pockets for a pen and notebook.

"Good, just listen. Do not try to remember. You need not write this down. My words will affix themselves in your mind. On that you may depend." Bridget stood and motioned for the man to remain seated. She walked to the sideboard and poured a very stiff Irish whiskey, handed it to Ahern, then she walked to the fireplace.

"You may, if you like, apologize and tell your master that these are the words I have dictated and you are not to be held responsible. Tell him also, there will be consequences if you are. I hope that makes you more comfortable."

With a weak smile, the man slumped in his seat on the white couch.

"I will help him with his existing difficulties and we will hear no more of his legislation. Ever. Again," Bridget said.

"Thank you, Mrs. Bragonier." Bridget held up her hand to quiet him and his eyes grew large as the words rang in his head.

*"Say the following to Mr. Connelly. Believe me, you will easily be able to recall my message word for word. Say only this, 'If ever you need my assistance Taoiseach, you are to come to me directly and in*

*person. If you ever – and I will repeat the word ever – threaten me or mine again, most assuredly, the cost to you personally will be higher than you can possibly imagine and certainly higher than those of your current predicaments.*

*"I do not threaten and I never bluff, Taoiseach. You crossed a very dangerous line when you drew my husband into this. Be assured, if you do this again, you will pray for your suffering to end quickly. I can assure you it will not."* Bridget completed her thought. Her mouth cut into a pleasant, but dangerous smile.

Bridget's eyes narrowed for a moment as another piece of her plan snapped into place. She switched back to the spoken word and her guest found that as alarming.

"Tell your master I will send him specific instructions on contacting an associate who can better address the problem. It would be best if Mr. Connelly did as he is directed," Bridget said with force and then in an instant, the heaviness in the room was gone.

"Tea or perhaps another whiskey?" she enquired with a glittering hostess smile.

\* \* \*

# CHAPTER SIX

A dejected thirteen witches returned to the police station at the south end of the village. "Mr. Maher," Lavonia said. "That Mrs. Hagan you sent us to see was very mean to us. She insisted she wasn't a witch and was, well, mean."

"Oi wouldn't pay her too much mind. It is just the sort of thing that a real witch would say to hide her identity, especially the evil, vile, nasty, vicious sorts of witches," Sean said with a vast smile. "Let's find you a better witch."

"Oi have it! You know the mayor, Thomas Cahill?" Sean asked and the witches nodded their agreement that they did.

"He's a witch?" Lavonia asked.

"Not a bit of it. Better." Sean leaned in and whispered, "Oi have it on good authority he is – you must remember, Oi never told you – he is a druid."

"A druid. Are you kidding?" an awestruck Lavonia Grayhawk asked. "We never dreamed we could meet an actual druid," and another witch from the back of the coven added, "And a real Irish one at that."

"Exactly, but Oi must warn you. He will try to hide his true identity too. Posing as a drunken lout who is our mayor because no one else will have the job is only a clever disguise." Sean dropped to a conspiratorial whisper. "Oi tell you, Oi've heard, Cahill is a druid among druids.

"His denials and pleadings are only a test of your resolve. To unlock his secrets, you must be persistent. Hound the man night and day. That's my advice," Sean said.

"Again, you must understand these are just things Oi've heard. Oi can't speak to the truthfulness of any of it," Sean concluded.

"Thank you, sir. You have been a huge help," Lavonia said and excitement and enthusiasm dripped from her pores.

"Think nothing of it. Believe me, the pleasure is all mine. We of the Gardaí are forever working with communities to protect and serve. All part of the job," Sean said and grinned a magnificent and maniacal grin.

*** 

A letter bomb went off in the general post office in Dublin on lower O'Connell Street. The explosion disintegrated nearby packages and shredded hundreds of letters. A blizzard of charred paper rained down on the stunned, and the dead.

A full minute passed after the blast before the injured began screaming. Few could hear the screams. Nearly everyone in the confined space of the sorting room had been rendered deaf. Some would recover. Some would not and the author of the bomb cared not at all.

The injured and the dead were just a horrific byproduct of the sender's mandate. The directive was a simple one. Sow terror and prosper or don't and don't.

The choice was his to make.

He made it.

* * *

"I know he is there. I know he is in pain. I can feel him, Moira. I must do something. I can't just sit and wait," Ailís said and pulled the bloom off a rose in Moira's garden.

"I miss him so, Moira," Ailís whispered.

"Must we go through this each and every time we meet? You are sorely trying my patience, lass," Moira said.

"When it's done you are, with your mushy, sad poor-me, let me know," Moira said. "Life is hard enough without you and your tale of hard luck.

"Ailís, it is important for you to be ready and nothing more. We do not know when he will return to us. It may be a day, a month or a year, but trust me, he will return. If he is what you want, you must be prepared to welcome him back into your life, aye and that of your son.

"Trust me, no matter the changes, you and Timothy are his life and this is his home. Know that and everything will be fine. Continue to mope around and 'tis a switch I'll take to you. Now, let's hear no more about this."

"But, Moira…" Ailís began.

"Witches and now you. Go cut me a switch!" Moira barked.

* * *

"Now, this is important, Finbar, ya nasty spawn of Satan. Out of me way. The squire is waiting to see Julian so he is coming with me and there are no two ways about it. Hold your evil on the inside 'til after we're gone, ya ugly little spud," Sean Maher said. He felt his instructors at the Garda academy would be proud. Their sensitivity training hadn't been lost on him.

Finbar Clancy said nothing, only inclining his head slightly as Julian materialized from the stand of bent and gnarled trees behind Sean.

"For the love of the good, sweet living Jasus! Julian Blessing! Oi knew nothing good would come from you associating with the likes of this, this, this creature!" Sean roared pointing at Finbar.

"Julian, you must come away with me now before Finbar Clancy can get his tentacles of evil around you. Believe me, he will squeeze the soul right out of you and leave you a husk of your former self. It can and will happen," Sean said as Finbar walked away chortling.

"Wasn't it Johnny Donavan who was healthy and whole until he ran into Clancy in the woods? Johnny is near unto a vegetable today. You need to put some distance between you and this place too. Dreary, Oi call it. It would depress a stoat," Sean said.

"Let's just get in the car and off we'll go to Cappel Vale right now. Why, with some good food and strong drink, we'll have you plumped up and feeling your old self in a twinkling. Please Julian, do this for a friend and for your own immortal soul. Fr. Fahey would tell you the same," Sean pleaded using the village priest's name to fortify his position.

"Sean," Julian began. "Finbar did not turn Johnny Donavan into anything. Odd as it may seem to you, alcohol turned Johnny into an alcoholic. Since he is drunk most of the time he only appears to be a vegetable."

"True, but 'tis that evil sod, Clancy, who drove poor Johnny to strong drink," Sean said.

"Finbar has no use for what is left of my soul, so we're safe there. As to the monastery, it suits my mood right now. I'm truly sorry, but for many reasons, I can't return to Cappel Vale with you. Believe me, I want to, but there is something I have to do first," Julian said.

"Now, to the squire. He isn't here for a social visit. Please return him to the village. He is up to something or he wouldn't be here. I want no part of it," Julian concluded.

"Now Julian," Sean chided. "You cannot say no to the squire."

"Okay, I'll say no to you and you can say no to the squire. I'm out of that business," Julian said.

"What business is that? You don't even know what the squire wants," Sean responded, his face carrying a twist of sincerity and hurt feelings. He thought it looked that way anyway. Julian thought it looked as though his big friend had tucked into a bad potato. "Besides, you and the squire are old and good mates. Oi just thought Oi would mention that in case you forgot."

"Sean, my friend," Julian whispered. "I am out of whatever business the squire has cooked up."

"But Julian," Sean began. "You can't say no, Oi already said you…"

"You already said what?" Irritation pulled Julian's mouth into a tight line before softening to a sad smile.

"Alright, for your sake I will go listen to that crafty old rascal. But this will be the last time I let you pull me into something like this, understood? Since he has roped you in, I will go and listen, but I promise nothing," Julian said.

"Last time," Sean said as he raised his hand. "On me sainted mother's grave. Last time."

"One more thing, Sean." Julian dropped his head and let out a noisy breath. "Your sainted mother is still alive."

* * *

Sean preceded Julian into Dr. Mahoney's study. He moved aside revealing Squire Lanigan, the last vestige of the Irish landed gentry. The man was a political force in several counties around Cappel Vale, and a wealthy landowner with the lives of the local residents at heart.

Shortly after arriving in Ireland, Julian and the squire met and arranged to play chess together regularly. They did their share of drinking too. That is the squire drank, frequently into oblivion, while Julian nursed his single malt. The older man was tall, reedy and in his seventies with an acidic tongue and the ready wit of a consummate curmudgeon. Married, estranged and reunited with the love of his life, Moira Hagan, made him a man who needed his wits about him at all times.

"Julian, lad, regardless of what that lummox Maher has told me, you look like hell." The squire didn't get out of the leather wingback chair, but extended his boney hand and looked genuinely pleased to see Julian.

"What is it you want of me, squire?" Julian's voice was almost painfully slow. A slight smile pulled the corners of his mouth up with effort.

The squire noted all of the changes he saw in Julian, changes for the worse. "Not even a how do you do? Well, boyo, since you're going to be so let's-cut-to-the-chase about it," the squire began, then added, "Bloody American". The old gentleman warmed to his task. "I find myself in an uncomfortable situation and the whole thing is a tangle. The short course is, I need your help."

If Julian was interested, his face hadn't received the memo. He stood and he waited.

"Yes, well. Here is the position," the squire harrumphed. "Some long while ago I had cause to seek out a politician. It was a very serious matter. I would never have done such a thing otherwise," the squire said with a heavy sigh. "So, I found my very good self indebted to said politico. Lay down with dogs, eh?

"I pay my own debts and always have," the squire said. "This time I've been boxed in. I owe this gentleman, as I said. He is now calling in the debt. Fair enough. Trouble is, inflation has to be considered. He has risen in the world as have I. I have more money and influence to spend and he has larger needs than when he was a nobody.

"The longer short course is, he popped up out of nowhere and asked for payment in a currency I don't have." The squire paused and looked troubled. "I've not spoken five words to the man in thirty years, then suddenly I am the man of the hour," the squire said.

"That's the way of it with politicians. They never forget the debts owed to them and never remember the debts they owe.

"Julian, he needs your special, well, let's say, skills. He has a problem that needs solving and what you do is what he needs.

"Trust me, son, I would never come to you like this with anything that wasn't dire." The squire let his hands fall into his lap and frustration etched itself on his face.

Julian asked, "And what about your wife? Moira was my teacher. She knows what I know."

The squire drew a noisy breath. "I went to her on bended knee. You see, the debt I incurred was because I was trying to get back at her those many years ago. I was angry and foolish and I did a stupid thing for which I've been furious with myself since. You made your home in Cappel Vale so you know the story."

"So she told you to come to me?" Julian's question was a whisper.

"No." The squire's answer was emphatic and left him looking bitter. "She said a few things. One was rather than help me with this, she would prefer to be found dead in a ditch. She is horrible at times," the squire said.

Julian looked at the floor and nearly smiled as he remembered how cantankerous his teacher had been with him.

"I suggested you and she dismissed the idea out of hand. I won't go into the details of what she had to say, but 'gritless', 'worthless' and 'eejit' were laid on with a trawl. I can say what she said was delivered with a snarl. I'm surprised you didn't feel it from here. That I came away with my skin was a minor miracle."

"Mrs. Bragonier then?" Julian inquired.

"I don't know her well, but I thought of that. Julian, this is political so you know it is low and filthy business. It will have to be dealt with in a ruthless fashion I'm sure. It's not that she is too genteel for the job. Truth of it is, what I know of her frightens me beyond reason, so there's that to consider.

"I tried to shield you with substitutions, but it is a no-go. No, son, the man asked for you by name. He knows of you. You are rather famous in certain circles. They are all ones I choose not to run in though."

Julian looked at and into the squire. There was no hint of deceit in the man. He had a problem and he came to Julian, desperate for assistance. Julian did sense the squire's heartfelt self-reproach at having to ask for help.

"This man, the one who holds your IOU, who is he and what is his problem?" Julian asked.

"He has two disasters on his hands. He assures me one could easily harm Ireland irreparably. The other he states is – his words – very literally a matter of life and death. That is all I know," the squire said.

"And," Julian prompted and the squire looked relieved.

"The goodly Garda Maher and I are to convey you in safety to Dublin whereupon we are to deposit you before no less a personage than our very own God rotting Taoiseach," the squire said.

"Julian, he is no better and frequently worse than most politicians, although occasionally he plumbs new lows." The squire grinned. "So, there is at least that for us to look forward to.

"I suppose when we get there, hijinks will ensue, so let's pack your kit and be gone," the squire said. "You'll be back within the day. I made him swear to that, but a politician's word is worth as much as his smile and is about as bankable. What say you, my boy? Will you help an old man?" the squire asked.

Julian thought a minute, shook his head, shrugged and said, "I have no idea what I can do for the man. However, for you I will go and at least listen. We'll see what happens from there."

\* \* \*

# Chapter Seven

Throughout the car ride to Dublin, the squire and Sean tried to initiate conversation, but Julian looked out the window from the back seat and said nothing.

The car entered Dublin proper and negotiated the dense traffic. Sean, who once recoiled from automobiles, was driving and enjoying himself as he ignored the heated shouts of others. Pedestrians and other drivers swerved and jinked to the curbs to avoid tearing metal or broken bones.

The car rocketed past the Upper Merrion Street entrance to the government buildings with their neoclassical architecture. Having sped past the unobtrusive gate beside the main government buildings, Sean applied the brakes forcefully. This served to jar Julian from his thoughts, elicited some choice curses from the squire and allowed Sean to make an illegal U-turn.

The gate guard referenced his clipboard, issued passes and gave Sean specific instructions as to where to park. They were instructions that were immediately disregarded. The three men moved into the side entrance of the main government building.

The Edwardian Baroque architecture instilled stability and commanded respect. The building complex was begun in 1903 through an act of the British parliament. It was completed in 1924. Pyramids were built in less time. British bureaucrats occupied the building just in time for the government of the newly formed Irish Free State to turf them out. Probably just a coincidence.

The squire, Julian and Sean walked down a thickly carpeted hallway and were ultimately directed to the office of the Taoiseach. The squire advised the waiting aid, Thomas Ahern, they were there for a meeting. Ahern asked the squire to take a seat, advising that the Taoiseach would be with them as soon as possible.

The wintery glare the squire issued sent Ahern scampering. Moments later Donald Connelly presented himself and welcomed his visitors, ushering them into his office.

Sean was content to remain in the outer office, but the squire unceremoniously pulled the far larger man out of his chair and into the meeting.

The Taoiseach's personal assistant, Edward Brennen, appeared and closed the doors behind them. Ahern and Brennen were glad to be done with them all.

Sean was stunned into silence at meeting the Taoiseach. This was a thing no Maher had ever dreamed possible. The squire looked wary, but intrigued. Julian was taciturn.

For an office of a head of government, the man's work space was simple. It belied the richness or vast expense of the carpet and the intricate design of the bleached oak furniture with its delicate, complex hand-worked walnut accents. Connelly asked the men to take seats and he assumed his position behind the desk.

"Gentlemen, it is ugly business we have before us, so I will speak without preamble. What I tell you now must not be spoken of outside this room," Connelly said. To an extent, this was added for melodrama since most of what he was about to say had already been reported in the newspapers.

Julian read in the man's racing thoughts his cunning, his arrogance and his fear. Right now, fear was ahead by several lengths.

The prime minister said, "There are two very different catastrophes at hand. First, there is a bomber on the loose. Gardaí headquarters sustained substantial damage and many lives were lost at an explosion in the central post office. They reportedly resulted from faulty gas lines. In fact, they were from letter bombs. The Archbishop of Dublin received one and now another has been received at Mansion House, the official residence of the Lord Mayor of Dublin. Those were intercepted before they could detonate. The main post office wasn't so lucky.

"The second disaster we have on our plate is state secrets and confidential operations and plans are being leaked to the mainstream media and other gossip mills. Doubtless, your fine selves have seen the stories in the papers.

"Both of these situations, if they are left to continue, will crush the public's faith in the government and lead to an upheaval in Irish life," the prime minister said. "That, gentlemen, does not even address the loss of life.

"Mr. Blessing, I believe you can bring this sad chapter to an end. I do not want to sound overly dramatic, but the safety and future of the Republic and the lives of its citizens is very much at stake," Connelly concluded.

Julian had formed his conclusions about the Taoiseach quickly and was listening to the dull ticking of an ornate clock in the corner.

He had sat in a far more ornate office in Rome not so long ago and listened to a similar clock. That one was in an office that ultimately saw a great deal of death and heartache. "People dead, the lives of others ruined…for what?" Julian asked himself for the thousandth time. He played the loop of those events and the thoughts twisted his mouth into an ugly slash.

With an effort, he returned to himself and realized the others in the room were looking at him. He sighed deeply and said in a laconic whisper, "Sir, what specifically do you want of me?"

Connelly watched Julian carefully, noting his impassive face accented by a scar running down his right cheek. The scar was the result of a beating Julian received when he first arrived in Ireland.

The report from the police stated Julian was caught unaware. With a politician's ability to read people, looking at Julian told the story. This was a man, regardless of his present condition, who would not be caught unaware again. Ever again.

The politician had to lean forward to hear Julian and was confused by his deathly slow cadence. In all, Connelly felt he was dealing with a man who wasn't living in the present. In fact, he thought he was dealing with a man who, although formidable still, was not living very much at all.

Connelly said, "We would like you to identify the persons responsible so that we might conclude this unpleasant business, of course."

"You have accounted for all the bombs?" Julian asked what seemed like a random question. The squire gave him a sidelong look.

"Naturally," Connelly said. "I have told you everything."

"Really?" Julian asked.

"Of course. What reason would I have to keep anything from you?" Connelly asked.

"I asked myself the same question. No matter. You have linked these events then?" Julian asked.

"The timing would support our conclusion," Connelly chuckled.

"But you have no solid evidence to support your supposition," Julian said. "What steps are you taking to find those responsible?"

"The most likely suspects are being," Connelly paused to consider, "monitored," he said. "As for the bomber, the Gardaí have every available man working on this to the exclusion of all else."

"And that has rendered what exactly?" Julian asked in a slow whisper.

"Mr. Blessing, the efforts of the government have, as yet, been inconclusive. We have endeavored to…"

Julian looked Connelly in the eye and said, "You have nothing."

The Taoiseach took a moment, smiled slightly and said, "Correct. We have expended a great amount of time, energy, manpower and money and, as you say, we have developed nothing."

The politician's face turned hard and unfriendly as he said, "Is it your plan to criticize our efforts or do you have something constructive to offer? I was led to believe we could expect great things from you." The man produced an artificial smile constructed entirely of distain.

Julian returned the look with a smile that was sad and distant. "Sir," he began, "you brought me here in order to help you. I was led to believe I should not expect anything from you at all. Thus far, you are delivering admirably."

The squire shifted uneasily in his chair and choked back a laugh while Sean Maher looked at the ceiling and pretended to be elsewhere.

The clock in the corner ticked.

Julian turned and looked at it.

The clocked stopped and they sat in silence.

Julian pressed his fingertips together. His gaze moved across Connelly's desk, up the man's shirt and lingered at the knot in his tie as it tightened slightly. He looked a little higher and his eyes locked on those of the politician.

Julian thought, and the man felt the words as they pushed him back in his chair and the air was sucked out of his lungs.

"*Taoiseach,*" Julian began. "*I will tell you only once. Do not test me and do not tempt me. And whatever you do, do not lie to me. I am not one of your constituents. Now, let's begin again, shall we?*" Julian released Connelly and looked away.

The clock began ticking and Connelly drew a breath he thought he might never draw again.

Julian returned to the spoken word. "You have received a letter bomb," Julian said simply.

The politician's nose flared and he waited.

"There has been an assassination attempt," Julian said softly, then cocked his head and his smile was sad and knowing. "I am sorry. I am wrong. Two attempts."

The breath Connelly let out was ragged. He handed a file folder to Julian. Without looking at it he passed it to the squire.

Julian continued to look into Connelly. The man's fear was palpable and rising. This was about assassination. It all depended on what kind. Political death via leaks or physical murder by way of bombs or bullets. To a politician, one was only slightly better than the other.

Aside from being blown to bits, nothing would stir a politician to the depths of fear Connelly was experiencing. Something was odd about the office, something skewed that lingered in the room.

"Sir," Julian said. "You believe the attempts to end your life and the assaults on your political career are linked. We may find that they are. Then again we may find they are not. The letter bombs that were sent to you may be part of the larger campaign. They may not be. I do not know the future. If I did, this would be a very short meeting.

"Since I don't have the second sight and I do not have the resources of a Garda Síochána, my ability to help is advisory only. If you will bring me any suspects you round up, I will tell you if they are viable candidates or not."

Without looking away from Connelly's face, Julian said, "As to the other, there I believe I can be of some assistance. The way you are looking at your watch and fingering that red portfolio, my guess is you have an important meeting to attend," Julian said.

"That's correct. It's a cabinet meeting I have in a few minutes."

"Good," Julian said. "Let's begin there. If looking for your enemies, looking at your friends and colleagues is a good place to start."

"A splendid idea," Connelly said with an enthusiasm he did not feel. "I will be happy to make introductions. As this is a cabinet meeting though, the things that are said are considered confidential and in some cases, secret or even top secret. Once the ministers take their seats around the table, you will have to leave."

The squire rubbed his forehead with two fingers and gave Julian another sidelong look. Being married to Moira Hagan, the squire knew what was about to happen. Sean knew something was about to happen, but had no idea what. He moved to the edge of his chair and waited.

The thought struck Connelly and pushed him back into his leather desk chair again. Julian's pale gray eyes locked on those of the Taoiseach as his smile turned sickly.

*"The squire and I will be staying for the duration of your cabinet meeting or for however long it takes me. Why is it I find myself threatening you when you brought me here to help? We are talking about your life. I thought you would be more interested."*

Connelly licked his pale lips, swallowed hard and said, "On second thought, Mr. Blessing, I've reconsidered. I see no reason why you and your friends can't attend and stay as long as you need to. My government is all about transparency."

The squire raised an eyebrow, snorted and otherwise looked bored.

"Introductions won't be necessary," Julian said. "We will attend your meeting and I will consider my impressions and give you answers when I have some. One additional item. Regardless of my success, the squire's obligation to you will be satisfied. Do I understand that correctly?"

"Oh, Mr. Blessing, Squire Lanigan owes me nothing. Never has," Connelly said and the squire rolled his eyes. "It is I who am indebted to him for his many years of support. Any small debt that may have been incurred has already been stamped 'paid in full'. Shall we, gentlemen?" a shaken Taoiseach said and led them out of the office. Mr. Brennen met them in the outer office and brought up the rear.

* * *

# CHAPTER EIGHT

Sean inserted his substantial frame between the squire and Julian.

"Julian, ya nearly kilt the man!" Sean said in a church-worthy whisper. "You've not changed a bit. You're still accomplishin' the devil's work and doin', well, well, things you oughtn't," Sean hissed. He didn't know what Julian did and didn't want to know. 'Devil,' 'Things,' and 'Oughtn't,' were all he needed to understand.

Julian, lost in his thoughts, said nothing.

Sean sighed deeply, but began to breathe heavily as he looked up and saw they were approaching the Cabinet Room.

"Maher," the squire said. "Do you see a need to attend this falderal? It's a room full of politicians talking gibberish. Not a place any but the worst type of Irishman wants to be. Why not take yourself down the street?

"A thousand years ago, when I used to come here often, a favorite place for some quiet contemplation was Doheny and Nesbitt on Baggot Street just down the way on the other side of Marrion. Bookmaker across the street, but I would stay out of there. Why not give us, oh, three beers should do it? Meet us back at the car," the squire said.

Sean looked up as each step brought him closer to politicians, gibberish and things he wasn't supposed to hear. In the other direction lay a pub and three beers.

Some decisions are easier to make than others.

* * *

The richly appointed Cabinet Room was a wonder of design. The conference table was enormous. An inset oval medallion, composed of scores of different shades of Irish walnut, showcased intricate marquetry. The black walnut band around the edge set off the white oak of the table and gave the room an air that blended artistry and power.

The table was fully equipped with data ports, docking stations and anything else the information technology department could think to incorporate.

High backed, leather upholstered chairs of exquisite design surrounded the table. Many of the chairs were occupied while other ministers refilled coffee cups and bartered for advantage with their colleagues at richly laid out side tables against the walls.

Julian and the squire were shown to chairs against a far wall. The Taoiseach took his place and the meeting began.

Julian took several deep breaths. His eyes became heavy lidded as he started to separate the individual signatures of those gathered. He learned to read people early in his development. Moira had encouraged him and it had come in very handy.

The room itself was a cacophony of conflicting emotions. Anger tending toward hatred was present as were envy and greed. Judging by the beltlines, gluttony was in attendance. There was the ever-present predisposition of politicians toward lust and pride. Judging by the bored looks, profound, nearly criminal laziness was much in evidence.

The Irish voters may or may not have been well represented, but the deadly sins were.

The meeting was called to order and pretense reigned supreme. Ministers pretended to be interested or concerned or inspired, but hardest of all, they acted as if they could tolerate each other.

Julian noticed almost nothing was getting done at a business level, but he continued to separate personalities. He assessed each looking for any sign, anything out of the ordinary. His problem was everything was out of the ordinary with these people.

There were those whose signatures were alive with malice, discontent, hatred, fear and animal cunning. He felt them all, read them all, catalogued them all. But throughout, there was a feeling. Something was off. Not fully wrong, but not quite right. He had felt it since he arrived.

In a room full of people whose every human emotion was skewed, there was an element either missing, that should have been there, or present that should not be. Julian pinched the bridge of his nose. The effort of protecting his own thoughts, while feeling those of others, was quickly draining him.

He had collected all he could, but was shocked he no longer had the reserves needed to go further if he had to. Although sitting, he sagged and leaned into the squire. The man noticed, but ignored it. He could feel how frail Julian had become. His friend was vulnerable, exposed.

"Politicians talking gibberish," the squire whispered. "We should have gone with Maher."

Julian nodded once and murmured, "I'm done." The men rose, Julian unsteadily, and without a look back, they left the room.

As the cabinet room door clicked shut, the Taoiseach thought he couldn't have planned it better. Not introducing Julian put a fox in the hen house. No further leaks, at least, could be expected for awhile.

The ministers would be busy scrambling to identify the unexpected visitor. The squire, they all knew. Now they had to figure out what they could trade the crafty old man to identify his pallid companion with the frightening stare.

* * *

But the Taoiseach was wrong. The ship of state was leaking like a sieve. The captain was in trouble and the crew was headed to the lifeboats. The only question remaining was when it would all turn turtle and sink.

Bloated appropriations documented, misappropriations cited, corruption named, scandals mentioned, graft suggested and sexual peccadilloes aplenty – the press had become a headline factory. Connelly could only sit by without comment and hope it all went away soon.

It wasn't going away soon.

* * *

The vehicle began to slow before sputtering to a stop. Sean coasted the car to the side of the road while the squire slept blissfully through the event.

"Julian," Sean said as his tone was at first artificially pleasant, "and it's you who did that, isn't it? Oi wish you would not do that sort of thing. By the wounds of Christ, ask me to stop the bloody car and stopped it will be!"

Unblinking, Julian continued to stare out the window of the car, eyes narrowed in concentration. "You were about to make a turn onto the road toward the village of Chapeltown. Let's just continue to the monastery, shall we?" He turned to his friend and continued. "It isn't far now."

"Julian, Oi was just going to stop for a wee moment to get a tiny nip of ale. It seems like we've been on the road for hours and not one jar have I had this day – well, except for the three beers. You could stay in the car with the squire and..."

Julian turned slowly to look his friend in the face. "Shall we continue on our way or would you like me to drive from over here?"

"You are a hard man, Julian Blessing, and play more than a bit rough with your friends."

* * *

"I'm sure you don't hear it often, but it is good to see you Finbar," Julian said on his return. The words came out softly and slowly, but carried a slight smile.

Finbar Clancy snorted and led the way from the cottages toward the headlands. "Sit, boyo and tell me of your visit to the big city and the wonders it had to behold," Finbar said and rubbed his hands together.

"Nothing much to report. I used to like cities. Dublin is like most other large cities – noisy and crowded with a lot of well-dressed people in a hurry."

"And?" Finbar said.

"A politician needed help with what he considered a serious problem or two. I went, I listened, I am back. Like I said, it was nothing," Julian explained with a lot of words that didn't explain anything.

"Well, if you're not going to tell me, I will tell you," Finbar said. "Keep in mind it takes no special talent to noodle out this puzzle.

"The squire is involved so the politician is an important one. The leader of our little country I would suppose. Few things could stir the squire to leave his manor house. Besides, every day, new revelations of shenanigans and naughty goings on are reported. At least that is what I understand. I don't soil my good self with newspapers and such like. Care to fill me in on the remainder?" Finbar asked.

"Nope, you've pretty much got it all. That's a good cold read, by the way," Julian answered.

"Julian, lad, why is getting information from you like pulling teeth?"

"Just part of my natural charm, I guess. Did I mention letter bombs? Yeah, that came up in conversation too," Julian said.

\* \* \*

Finbar and Julian walked along the headlands fronting the Irish Sea. Storm clouds scudded across the sky in the distance. Julian had a newspaper under his arm.

"So, your plan is to do nothing? Do I have that right, Julian?" Finbar demanded. "Would you agree Manning is at the bottom of this bombing business?"

"I have no doubt," Julian answered.

"A man obviously interested in attracting your attention snuffs out some lives and your response is what?" Finbar shouted.

"Nothing, yes, that is exactly my response," Julian whispered. "If Manning and Clarke want me, they can find me easily enough. I have no intention of going out looking for them. That will only put more innocent lives at risk. For all of that, you may want to clear out and take the doctor with you. What are you grinning at?" Julian said with force.

"You, son. That is about as good an answer as could be given in the current circumstances," Finbar said with a smile of purest satisfaction.

"The natural response would be to go hunting Manning and Clarke. That would be satisfying in that it would quickly give you the revenge you want. However, the cost of revenge is always high. You are right in thinking innocents would be caught in the crossfire and that is an unacceptable price for the justice you seek," Finbar said. "Besides, you're not ready.

"Here is something for you to think on," the little man continued. "We all accept there are seemingly two very different realities. However, for the most part, we all use our talents in the same way. When fighting the darkness, attack begets defense begets attack. Each attack escalates the level of violence until either the darkness or the light prevails, no?" Finbar said.

"What if there was another way to exercise our gifts?" Finbar asked.

The old man smiled as he turned and walked back to his cottage leaving Julian to look out onto the green black Irish Sea and consider.

* * *

"What?" Thomas Cahill, the nominal mayor of Cappel Vale asked.

"We have reason to believe you are a druid," Lavonia said.

"What?"

"No sense denying it. Your disguise may fool others, but not us. We are here to learn and, now that you have been confronted, it is your job to teach us." She stated her case with practiced ease due mainly to the sheer number of times she had practiced making it.

"What?" Mayor Cahill's head hurt. It always hurt in the early morning before a nice breakfast Guinness. This morning, standing between him and morning fortification, he had a large deputation of witches saying things that made no sense.

"Now," Lavonia said, "what would you have us do first, Master Cahill? Or is that Master Thomas? What do people call druids?" Lavonia asked in rapid fire.

"What?" the mayor asked.

"Why do you keep saying 'what?'" Lavonia demanded.

Another member of the coven piped up. "It is obviously some trick to throw us off, wear us down so we will cave and go away."

"Well, that isn't gonna work, mayor. You can say 'what' all you want, but we aren't going to give up. We know you for the druid you are and you are going to teach us whether you like it or not so just stop saying 'what'."

"Why are you doing this to me??!!" the mayor wept.

* * *

"Do you agree Rome changed you?" Finbar asked Julian as they walked along the headlands facing the sea.

"Of course," Julian replied.

"Do you suppose your current state of healing has changed you further? I'll answer for you – indeed it has," Finbar said. "You assume it changed you by making you less. Perhaps it only made you different than you were before. Is that a possibility, son?" Finbar asked.

He continued. "Isn't now a good enough time to invent your fine self again and get that girl of yours and make a life for yourselves?" Finbar asked and drew on his pipe.

"Finbar," Julian said. "Finding a new life, any life for that matter, isn't in the cards for me yet. I have something that has to be done before any of that is even possible."

"Aye, but that doesn't answer the question, now does it?" Finbar said.

"You ask too many questions," Julian said.

"And you answer too few," Finbar replied.

\* \* \*

Julian took up a punishing regime. Early mornings he spent in spiritual exercises. Meditation had served him when he worked with Moira. He started again but this time he followed the glimmer of hope Finbar offered. Perhaps there was just enough of him left that he could invent himself again. He had done it once before when he came to Cappel Vale.

He came from an insanely hectic life in New York City to the gentle pace of rural Ireland. The village had given him friends, a woman who loved him without condition, a mentor, a teacher, an array of talents he didn't know he possessed and a life worth living.

Maybe it was possible to make all that happen again. Maybe. If he survived.

And possibly there was a way of wielding his talents differently. He had thought only in terms of attack and defense as Finbar said. That is what his teachers taught, because that is what they knew, but the Jesuit Book had opened doors and hinted at options and alternatives. What if?

He focused his mind and then began the process of trying to empty it of all but what was important, what was true.

\* \* \*

"Chief Superintendent Murphy, they said you wanted to see me?" Inspector Flannigan asked his boss' boss' boss.

"Flannigan, the man of the hour. Come in. Take a seat," Murphy, a decorated and seen-too-much career police officer said.

Flannigan thought nothing good was going to come from this visit. He was nearly right.

"There is a person sitting in my outer office. You noticed of course," Murphy said.

"Yes sir. Older, thin, pale skin, brown hair…"

"What is this 'older' business! Since the man is substantially younger than me, I take some exception with your characterization of his age," Murphy said and cocked an eyebrow.

"Yes sir. Sorry sir," the inspector said. "Older than me, would be a better way of looking at it."

"Yes, well, you saved yourself that time. In any case, you'll be working with him on this bombing case. His name is Julian Blessing and he comes to us by way of no less than the Taoiseach." The Chief Superintendent was less than enthused.

"Does this man know something? How can he help us? Why has Mr. Connelly put him onto us?" Flannigan asked.

"What this Blessing brings to the table is anyone's guess." In a sardonic aside Murphy added, "I didn't think to question the Taoiseach's motives.

"No worries, lad. Go introduce yourself to our visitor. Offer him whatever assistance we can within reason. When you have discovered the answers to all the questions you just asked, let me know. Good, luck. That will be all," Murphy said.

\* \* \*

"Finbar," Dr. Mahoney said as the two men walked beside a stone wall dividing the monastery from the adjoining farmer's pasture.

"I'm afraid, from my point of view, Julian has been dealt a bad hand," Dr. Mahoney said.

"It is the hand he has been dealt, doctor. It is for him to play it. The choices he makes are his choices. There is little we can do to help him, I'm afraid," Finbar said.

"And if he loses?" the doctor asked.

Finbar Clancy nodded his head. Both men knew the outcome.

* * *

Flannigan, a pragmatic young detective with a view to a future in police work, approached Julian and extended a hand.

"Mr. Blessing, I'm Inspector Flannigan. We'll be working together. I will be your liaison for anything the Garda can provide."

"It is a pleasure to meet you, Inspector," Julian said. The handshake was firm equalizing Julian's grip. It was neither too strong nor too weak, but a mirror image of Julian's.

He looked into the younger man and what he saw made him smile. "How did you get so lucky to draw this assignment?" Julian asked.

"It was thought I was the best man for the job," Flannigan answered and Julian knew it for the prevarication it was.

"So, nobody else would have the job or they otherwise suddenly became too busy?" Julian asked.

Flannigan considered a moment and answered, "Sir, being the only man available for the job, I became the best man for the job. I'm junior in the department, so…"

"I understand," Julian said slowly. "Let's see what kind of success we can make of this then."

"Sir, if you don't mind my asking, what is it you do?" the inspector asked.

"There is a lot of debate about that," Julian answered.

\* \* \*

All the window glass from the ultra-modern hotel lobby had been blown into the road in the trendy Ballsbridge section of Dublin. Furniture had been turned to kindling and large chunks of the marble floor had been turned into shrapnel.

Remarkably, no one had been in the hotel at the time.

The evacuation had been an orderly one and all the guests and staff were assembled two blocks away on Pembroke Road on a rainy, bitter night in Dublin.

The bomb had detonated one hour later. It all transpired as the caller said it would.

Inspector Flannigan knelt near a shallow crater while Julian walked among the broken ruminants of the large central chandelier and modern wall sconces.

Flannigan approached Julian and said, "The bomb squad said it was the same as the other pipe bombs –rudimentary, but efficient and not enough remains to analyze beyond the explosives residue.

This one was smaller than the others. The thinking is it was easier to conceal. It is thought it wasn't meant to do as much damage as some of the others."

"The message seems clear enough. He can do this anytime, anywhere," Julian commented in his slow whisper.

"And with or without warning," the inspector added.

"I can't see anything here outside of the loss of life and destruction that could have been," Julian said. His shoulders dropped and his eyes opened slowly. He looked to Flannigan more drained than fatigued.

"Pardon me, sir. Are you a psychic or something?" Flannigan asked.

"Or something," Julian answered and added, "I'm sorry, inspector, but could you drive me to where I'm staying? It is a ways out of Dublin, but I'll give you directions. I'm just so terribly tired suddenly."

* * *

Meditation followed by discussion followed by practice. Julian began to rebuild. He had yet to determine what he would become, but with Finbar's gentle shepherding he was changing.

His gestures, his walk, his talking all took on a more relaxed tenor. Thoughtful before, he was more self-aware now, more reflective and more accepting.

Never far from his mind were his ghosts, the bombings, the government leaks and Ailís. Thoughts of her were his only respite, his only refuge.

Although the acceptance began with others, more importantly, Julian was beginning to accept himself, his new self. He was beginning to trust his instincts and feelings again.

During a morning discussion with Julian, Finbar said, "Julian, me lad, you are strong and getting stronger. I still feel your soul is suffering from your need to settle the problem of revenge," Finbar said.

"It has taken a lifetime for you to become who you are today. Sad I am to tell you, you will move no further and learn no more until you fall back to the basics of who and what you wish to be."

The little man continued, "What controls you, son? Is it fear, hope, hate, love? The anger and shame you feel, that's natural. How you act on those things is learned. You must put away what you know and look inside for what is truest about you."

Julian thought and Finbar felt the words. *I don't know what is real, what is true, what is false. My entire world is made up of gray tones right now. There is no clear line separating the dark from the light anymore.*

"Our people often think the greatest danger is found when they enter the dark," Finbar said. "They are wrong. The most peril is found where you stand right now. Now is the time to trust yourself and put away all you have learned about being," Finbar said.

"You know as well as I do what the problem is. You practice daily and you are never satisfied with half measures. But you are seeing the practice of your talents as a thing separate from who you are. The same is true of your meditations. You feel you don't know who you are and so are searching. I tell you, you have found it," Finbar said with force.

"I don't understand," Julian said and confusion and frustration clouded his pale gray eyes.

"Your talents are not a thing apart. They are not even a part of you. Don't you understand, lad? Your talents are you. Everything you want, everything you need, everything you are or will ever be is to be found in using your skills," Finbar said.

"Before you can go farther though you must know you are more than the physical substance you see. You exist in two worlds. One world is shrouded in the mist of misunderstanding and outright falsehood. The other world is the one where all things are possible, a world illuminated by the light of understanding."

Finbar stopped, drew on his pipe and waited as he watched Julian struggle with life's thorniest concepts – the physical versus the metaphysical, the normal and the paranormal, the corporeal and the incorporeal.

\* \* \*

"Momma, Mr. Maher says to come quick and Mrs. Hagan too!" Timothy Dwyer shouted.

The women were standing in Moira's garden when Timothy ran up. "Slow down, son," Moira said. "There's nothing that is all that important that we can't take a minute to collect ourselves."

"Tell us what you know," Ailís said.

"Some of the visitors ran to get Mr. Maher. A witch had been found dead."

"Lead the way, boy. We haven't got all day," Moira said and snatched up her shawl.

# Chapter Nine

A young man in a conservative business suit sat at a high marble table across from the gracefully curved mahogany bar. The place was Searsons of Baggot Street near Waterloo Road in Dublin.

He looked like a half dozen other patrons in the 1920's style pub with its skylights, art deco accents and air of jovial business dealings.

Finishing his drink, the young man set his glass on the table, nodded to the barman and left by the front door. He left behind a brief case and so much more. He left behind death and devastation.

\* \* \*

The scene was a mass of witches, all angling for a view of the body. Once they had attained that, with few exceptions, they started vomiting.

Ailís led the way into the crowd, but Moira decided jostling a lot of overheated foreigners was more then she could tolerate.

"Clear a path and clear it now," Moira hissed and a path through the center of the gathering formed. All noise came to a halt.

"Thanks for that," Ailís said.

"My pleasure," Moira answered as they hurried to Sean's side.

Ailís stopped short and turned to find her son staring at the body. They still had a distance to go, but Timothy had come far enough.

"Enough excitement for one day, Timothy. Off with you. There is nothing for you to see," Ailís said.

Lying on the river's edge was the body of a man in his early twenties with a slight frame. Blond hair lay matted across his forehead and into eyes open and staring. The color of his skin was nearly the same blue as his robe and cloak.

"What do you have, Sean?" Ailís asked as she approached.

"This one was fished out of the river. The body got hung up on some tree roots. If not for that, he may have washed out to sea. Don't know how long he has been in the water. Oi had him laid out so you could examine him. Fell in and drown Oi would say. All that wool he is wearing would have weighted him down. A strong man couldn't swim in that getup. This boy? Never," Sean speculated.

"Oi've not started interviewing people yet. Oi'll need to call headquarters in Dundalk. Oi'm sure they will want to send a medical examiner to take the body away. That is unless you want to do the autopsy," Sean said to the doctor.

"Not me. Don't be daft. They are set up for this sort of thing. Moira, do you want to add anything?" Ailís said including her companion.

"Been in the water for a fair bit, but not overly long. Could have drown, but something doesn't feel right about that," Moira said.

"What doesn't feel right about it to you?" Sean asked.

Moira bent over for a closer look. "Don't know, it just doesn't feel right. The Hacketts might know something. They usually do."

"Sean, you call your people and send the crowd on its way. I'll stay with the body until the authorities arrive," Ailís said.

\* \* \*

Sean roared and the crowd dispersed. From the police station, he made his call and returned to the riverbank with the Hackett sisters, owners of the village apothecary.

Ailís stepped aside and the sisters examined the body. These were women who could dispense medications, poultices and advice with accuracy and occasional compassion. They spent an inordinate amount of time with the victim's face and hands and chest.

They looked at each other and nodded. "Poisoning," they said in unison.

"So he didn't just fall in and drown?" Sean asked.

"Poisoning," both sisters said again with irritation.

"Do you know what poison was used?" Sean asked.

Each sister considered a moment. They stood, smoothed out their identical long black skirts, adjusted their matching black jackets and said, "Wolfsbane."

"The sort of thing a witch would use, no?" Ailís asked.

"That is probable. A foreigner to be sure. Wolfsbane doesn't grow in Ireland," one sister said.

"Are you sure?" Sean asked and Ailís closed her eyes.

The Hacketts crossed their arms over their ample breasts and cocked an eyebrow apiece.

"Oh," Sean said. "Sorry Oi asked. Just went stupid for a moment."

"For a moment?" one Hackett asked. The other cocked another eyebrow.

Ailís shook her head. Some people never learn.

* * *

"Julian, I have visions sometimes. Over the years I've come to trust them. If I see it happen, it happened or will happen," Finbar explained.

"I take it this isn't just general information," Julian said.

"Your parcel has been taken," Finbar said. "I don't know how I know. What I know is a package belonging to you has been stolen. I only saw flashes, momentary images. Nothing more. Your property, a bank safety deposit box and someone taking the package out who wasn't you – that is what I saw, no more."

"It could have been any safety deposit box, any package, but it wasn't," Finbar said with a shrug. "Obviously, this means something to you."

"It means Manning is about to become unhappy. I trust that unhappiness will lead to missteps on his part," Julian said.

"Tell me about your package, your book, Julian."

"What book?" Julian asked.

"Listen, son, an object like that is not going to remain hidden for long. There have been rumors of such a thing for centuries. Most ignore the legends in the hope that a book like that doesn't exist. For that reason, it takes its place in the world of myth. It's true though, isn't it?" Finbar asked in a near whisper.

Julian considered for a moment then slowly said, "Yes, it's true. It was compiled in secret over many different eras, by many different people and many have given up their lives to protect it," Julian said.

"We can assume Mr. Manning has possession of this book then?" Finbar asked.

"We can assume he has possession of the book from my safety deposit box."

Finbar's ancient gray eyes narrowed. "Is that the question I asked?" he said.

"I don't know, is it?" Julian asked.

* * *

Moira was working in her garden busily pruning roses. She could feel them, they were near and they were about to do something stupid.

She turned quickly and stared down another deputation of witches. "State your business and then be gone," Moira said.

"Good day, milady. We have come in search of Mayor Cahill," a tall male witch said.

"Don't think for a moment I am a lady, yours or anyone else's. However, do tell me when you find the mayor. I have something for him." And she began snapping her pruning shears with an unhealthy vigor.

* * *

"Tell me how you came to be here," Julian asked Dr. David Mahoney.

"Oh, it is a boring story really," the doctor said.

"You have asked me to repeat my story to you often enough. Bore me with yours," Julian said.

"Well, I was someone at one of our premier hospitals. In fact, Dr. Dwyer was a resident toward the end of my time there. I was constantly busy. I suppose I liked it that way because it distracted me from life," the doctor began. "You could say life and death kept me from living life."

"One day, a man breezed into my office and told me it was time to go. I had a vague recollection of the fella, but couldn't quite place him. Still, I knew I knew him.

"I remember it as if it was yesterday. 'State your business then get out. I have things to do,' I said. Arrogant I was then as well as stupid," the doctor said.

"Bold as all that, the man said, 'You have work to do and that work isn't here. Leave your things and come with me,'" the doctor said and smiled along with a pleasant memory.

"For some reason it fell into place. 'I know you,' I said. Indeed, the man had been chief of surgery back in the day when I was a resident. You can imagine that was when dinosaurs roamed the earth." The doctor chuckled and Julian smiled.

"In any case he told me I had important work to do. He said anyone could do my job, but the work he had for me was something only I could do. For some reason I got up and followed the man. I didn't have any family and my work was my life, so I wasn't giving up much.

"He brought me here and here I have remained ever since. That would have been twelve years ago. I can tell you, in the early days, I didn't believe much of what I saw and any of what I was told. Over time, he and his patients wore me down and made me who I am today.

"One day, I woke up to find the old man had vanished. I was in charge. You know, at the end of the day, I found both the life I lived and the work I had been doing weren't really all that essential. I feel the work I do today is important because my patients are important.

"That isn't to say those patients aren't a stubborn lot. Fortunately, they aren't all as difficult as you, my boy. In fact, none of them have been." The doctor laughed and Julian smiled again his slight smile.

\* \* \*

"You have the look of a man who has made progress of the wrong sort. Either that or you ate something that didn't agree with you," John Clarke said and smiled a forced smile at his mentor.

"In fact, I have. Made progress of the wrong sort, that is," Manning said.

"You have the Book I see. That is capital. How was it done?" Clarke said as he moved closer to the slim volume on Manning's desk.

"It was simple really," said the older man. "Blessing had the Book put in a safety deposit box in the safest bank in Ireland. I stood one of the bank directors to lunch and asked him to bring me the Book. He refused at first. Said it wasn't possible.

"All things are possible, as they say. Once I obliterated his mind, he was a puppet. In short, he found a way to access the deposit box. He brought me the Book, but sadly, he did not survive our encounter. Lunch was quite good though."

"Poor chap," Clarke said without feeling. "And that is it?"

"John, John, John, of course. Here you are," and the Book, seemingly of its own accord, slid easily across the Manning's desk to his protégé.

Clarke dropped any pretense of a pleasant expression as he thumbed through the leather bound copy of Little Women. The book showed its age and felt buttery soft, worn smooth by hundreds of hands. "Well, isn't Mr. Blessing a clever boy? Sadly, not even a first edition."

Manning's broad smile fell away quickly. "Blessing has caught us out and for that he will pay. One does not play me for a fool with impunity.

"He could never have come so far so fast without the contents of the Jesuit Book. The Book is vital, to be sure, but Blessing is more important now since, in any case, he still has what we want."

"My opinion is we eliminate him," Clarke said and his manner was matter-of-fact.

Manning thought for a moment. "It was my hope we could keep this simple, but such is not going to be the case. Blessing proved formidable in Rome. I thought at first it was his friend Fr. Soski who was aiding him. That did not turn out to be the case.

"No, Blessing is talented and unpredictable. The man has a gift for doing the unexpected with disturbing regularity. Terminating him will not be easy. Terminating him and getting our hands on the Book will be impossible."

"I thought you said, 'all things are possible'," Clarke said with a sardonic smirk and Manning said nothing.

Clarke looked out the window and thought, *I understood after Rome he was a spent force. Have I been misinformed?*

"*Yes and no,*" Manning thought. "*Rome left him badly damaged and if he were any man I would say 'spent' would be a good description. Mr. Blessing is not just any man, John. He is formidable, and I feel the contents of the Book quadrupled his ability to be dangerous. His association with Finbar Clancy will only speed his growth.*"

"*But we have intelligence that says any growth on his part has come to a stop,*" Clarke thought and looked concerned.

"*I don't believe it. That is, I can't afford to believe it. Clancy wouldn't have been brought in for no reason and Blessing is not the sort of man who gives up. I underestimated him in Rome. I won't make that mistake again,*" Manning answered.

The older man considered the relative value of whether Julian lived or died. Having decided, he compartmentalized the problem, dismissed the matter and moved along to more pressing business.

To Terrance Manning, the lives and deaths of others were a small matter indeed.

He smiled.

The smile was not a smile at all.

\* \* \*

# Chapter Ten

The silence of the monastery's chapel was nearly palpable. The air was close and smelled of wet stone and dust. Most of the pews had been removed long ago leaving the stone communion rail and the steps leading to the altar for company. Mounted high on the altar was an ancient tabernacle, blackened with age and with a Celtic cross affixed to the door. Here was a building which last saw services half a century ago.

"The choices are fairly clear, Julian," Finbar said as he and Julian walked up the center of the nearly vacant space. "Either Manning will come to you or you will go to him. Have you changed your mind? Which will it be?"

"He will come to me or, should I say, for me? Either way. He will come right to where we are standing," Julian whispered.

"You are so sure?" Finbar asked.

"I am sure. He will come here," Julian said.

"Manning has been around a long time. He is cunning, powerful and vicious, a potent combination. It will take all we have to destroy him," Finbar said, "and destroy him we must. Choosing the battleground is a good strategy."

"Finbar, two things are wrong with that. First, there is no 'we'. This is something I will do by myself. I don't want to involve you in any of this. Enough people have died already. This is between Manning and me. Second, I have no intention of destroying him," Julian and smiled slightly.

* * *

"Sean Maher," Fr. Fahey said. The priest was a man of slight stature and a huge presence. He was old, but his true age was impossible to guess. He had been at St. Michael's Catholic Church for nearly thirty years, but even that was open for debate.

"Yes father," Sean answered sheepishly. "And how are you this fine morning?"

"Thomas Cahill has taken refuge in the church. He claims he is beset by devils. You wouldn't be knowing anything about that, of course?" the priest asked.

"Devils, Father?" Sean replied. "Of devils Oi know almost nothing. Are you sure Cahill doesn't have the drink on him? He usually does this time of day. Any time of day actually."

"Oddly enough, he is currently paying for his sins by being sober. Oi had to lock up the altar wine just to be safe, although one can never be too safe. One can't be too careful. In any case, he is on about devils and witches and he says you put them on him. If so, please remove them so Oi can have my church back," the old man said.

"Good father, Oi am afraid we are, as you well know, waist deep in witches. Speaking of which, have you checked with the Hagan? Putting a devil on Cahill would be just the sort of thing she would do," Sean said and then continued.

"Although Oi don't hold with witches, in this case Oi feel the Hagan would probably be justified in putting a hex on Cahill. No one so richly deserves it. Did you know he is selling maps to the 'holy places'? And Oi don't mean St. Michael's church," Sean said.

"All very nice, Maher," the priest said. "But Oi'll not be thrown off the track so easily. Did you or did you not put a load of witches on Thomas Cahill." As the priest phrased it, it wasn't really a question.

"As a good Catholic, Oi can say Oi did not and am offended, aye and a wee bit vexed, you accused me of such a despicable act no matter how much Cahill deserves it."

"Well, Oi can see Oi'll get no straight answers from you this day. Oi see you said 'a good Catholic', which you are not, since there is nothing a'tall good about your form of religion, but it saved you from a lie told to a priest," Fr. Fahey said. "Oi will see you on Saturday at confession."

"That you will, although Oi have only a tiny sin or two to confess," Sean said.

"Maher, your soul is little more than a bucket of mortal sin," the priest said and marched off toward his church to make sure his altar wine hadn't been violated.

✳ ✳ ✳

Sean rushed to Ailís' office home. Bursting in he said, "Oi got the report from the medical examiner's office. Those nasty Hackett sisters were wrong just as Oi thought," Sean said, overflowing with glee.

"Oh, and what did the medical examiner have to say?" Ailís asked, her brow knotted in interest.

"The victim, one Edward Biggins, did die of poisoning but not what the loony Hacketts said it was."

"I will ask again, because I am in a charitable mood. What did the medical examiner have to say?" Ailís asked, this time more annoyed then interested.

"Ha! The poison was Aconitum!" Sean-the-Victorious said and followed it with, "Ha!" again for good measure.

"Sean?" Ailís said.

"Right, Oi'm going to go right over there and tell those two that they don't know everything. Oh sure, they can lord it over the rest of us with their ointments and their…" Sean said.

"Sean, I would advise against that," Ailís said.

"Oh sure, all of you in the medical business stick together. Should have known, but Oi expected better of you, doctor."

"Sean?" Ailís said.

"Why do you keep saying me name? Ha! Just trying to save them from the tongue lashing Oi'm going to deliver!"

"Aconitum is wolfsbane," Ailís said. "It is also called aconite, monk's hood, leopard's bane, mouse bane, women's bane and devil's helmet. I looked it up."

"Oh," Sean said.

"Hmmmm," Sean said.

"Umm," Sean said.

"Well, that doesn't mean they know everything about everything," Sean said with a conviction he did not feel.

"For the sake of your health, I wouldn't mention that to them," Ailís said.

\* \* \*

"Tell me about this place," Julian said one afternoon as he and the doctor walked the verdant hillsides.

"The monastery? Well, more is not known about it than is. It has been here for some time. It was the home to an order of monks. No one I know is sure of who they were. The place is said to date from the year 1242. The residents could have been Benedictines, Cistercians, Dominicans or Carmelite friars.

"Did you know there were Knights Templar in Ireland? This place didn't belong to them which is a shame. It would give my stories a great deal more color.

"Whoever they were, they managed to frighten the hell out of the locals. The place has been abandoned for centuries, but not a stone has been removed from the place. Usually, when the monks move out, the local farmers start taking stones for fences and housing. Not so here.

"I actually foster the nonsense. I never confirm or deny it of course, but," the doctor affected a stage whisper, "druids to be sure."

"What? You encourage the local population to believe we're druids? No one is sure if druids even existed," Julian said.

"Well, never tell an Irishman that. They love their folklore and superstitions. Besides, it serves to keep people away while increasing my standing in the community," the doctor laughed.

"It is rather a perfect life I have here. I get interesting cases like yours and I can practice being a country doctor as well. That is the sort of medicine I signed on for, but sadly got caught up in our national healthcare bureaucracy. Sad really, but I'm making up for my past transgressions.

"You know, it is popular belief that the druids could draw energy from the very stones. The old religion gave way to the new. The older one is far more interesting," Dr. Mahoney said.

"Oh well, I still favor the Knights Templar version," the doctor concluded.

"Doctor, what has changed for you recently? You are on edge, nervous," Julian said. He wanted to use the word panicked, but held back.

"Me? Nothing really. These bombings might have me edgy. That is horrible business. The man in the village who was killed, that has me terribly upset. His murderer was so callous, so, I don't even know what words to use to describe taking a life in so cold a manner."

Julian watched as the loop of past events played before him. There was Clarke, well-groomed as ever. A jovial farmer approaches the bar. He says something. Clarke turns slowly, his eyes go hooded. The farmer clutches his chest and is dead before he hits the ground.

Julian's ability to see past events clearly had been a help and a hindrance. His lip curled involuntarily as he watched Clarke step over the body and leave the pub. He watched it happen a score of times. Each time made him sick. And angry.

# Chapter Eleven

"Julian, old son, there is something I want you to understand," Finbar began. The two men were sitting on the remains of a broken stone wall facing a verdant pasture where a few disinterested cows were grazing.

"Know I appreciate the suffering you've been enduring and the resiliency you've shown. Why, it is very few indeed who could rise from the ruins of a ravaged life as you have," Finbar said. "To be sure, you're not there yet, but substantial progress has been made.

"For some odd reason you don't want me to see you struggle with your demons. Understand and accept I have seen such battles waged by so many others. I know the look of 'em and can spot 'em at a distance.

"What you have done, Julian, is little short of astonishing. Through a supreme force of will, you are well on the road to recovery of yourself. That is no insubstantial feat. I have watched many try and fail. I've seen many others turn away from the challenge and give up.

"You have been knocked down many times since I've been here. Each time you get up and try again. It takes a special kind of person to do what you've done, what you are doing.

"I just wanted you to know, your efforts have not gone unnoticed. You are making progress and it is coming faster than you can see," Finbar said.

After a thoughtful silence, Julian took in a deep breath of sea air, and said, "I appreciate what you're saying. Still, as fast as progress is coming, it is not fast enough. Manning and Clarke will be coming sooner than any of us know."

"Speaking of going unnoticed, we are being watched again," Julian said.

"Yes, I know," Finbar answered. "It's why we're here flapping our gobs and looking vulnerable."

* * *

"John, this has to stop. Blowing things to bits is getting us no closer to our goal," Manning said.

"I was about to say the same thing to you," Clarke answered quickly and with force.

"What do you mean?" Manning asked.

"You keep blowing up any and all establishments with no thought to the strategic value of said targets. Where exactly are you going with this and why do you keep accusing me?" Clarke said.

"You are telling me you have nothing to do with these bombings?" Manning asked.

"That is exactly what I am telling you. Do you expect me to believe you have nothing to do with them?" Clarke asked.

Both men thought for several minutes in silence accented by the crackling wood fire.

"Find out who is doing this and bring him to me. Use whatever resources you need," Manning said with a sneer.

\* \* \*

Francis Mulherin of Mulherin's Pub presented himself at the police station in Cappel Vale. He was unhappy. Unhappy was a natural state of affairs for Francis, but this time he was really unhappy.

"Why so glum, you dreadful little man?" a chipper Sean Maher called from the recesses of the station.

"Witches," Mulherin said wiping his shoes before he entered.

"Ah yes, it is a keen eye you have, Francis. Witches we have in abundance. The good news is, with luck, they will dilute the evil of our own resident witch, eh?" Sean said.

"Right now, I'll take the Hagan anytime to the load of loons we have on our hands," Mulherin said and crossed himself.

"What afflicts you can be cured easily. Let us repair to your pub and jam our noses into a nice jar of the black stuff."

"That's the problem, ya eejit," Francis said with some heat. "I can't go near me own pub for all the witches who are hounding me and where me nephew is probably robbing me in a hundred ways, only fifty percent of which I will ever uncover."

"'Tis a great sadness that is, Francis me boy. Tell me, why is your filthy little pub awash in witches?" Sean asked.

"Your guess would be as good as mine. There I was minding me own business when, without warning, this score of witches show up with the damnedest story," Francis answered. "Except, it isn't a story. They stated it as fact when it is nothing but a filthy lie.

"Seems they are convinced I am a druid or some such drivel. What puts such thoughts into a person's head? Do they just pick some citizen at random and declare them all manner of things? What kind of person does that?" Francis asked.

"Hmmm," Sean said and continued, "Oi can state without any hesitation, you, Francis Mulherin, are definitely not a druid, although Oi can't speak to the some such drivel part," Sean said.

"I'll thank you for that at least, but it is help I need to rid myself of these witches."

"Oi would like to help you solve this mystery, but alas, solving mysteries is thirsty work. Oi know. We'll take ourselves off to O'Gavagan's Pub to quench our thirst for justice," Sean said.

"Oh, that's right. Let's go to O'Gavagan's. Ya great fool! If you hadn't noticed, O'Gavagan is a competitor of mine and, since he dropped his prices, a scoundrel likely to leave me and me family destitute."

"Ah, the sacrifices Oi make to protect and serve my little community. Alright, we'll puzzle this one out and not a drop will be drunk," Sean said.

"There is no solving this riddle. I am doomed to be plagued by witches, driven from me own establishment, constantly forced to hide, beg for scraps of food, be shunned by those who once loved me and live in a box behind O'Gavagan's where drunks will probably piss on me little cardboard house," Francis, a man in moderate despair, sobbed.

"Yes indeed, no one truly enjoys misery like an Irishman, eh?" Sean said. "Let's get back to your problem. We'll look at this scientifically like the Gardaí teach.

"Chances are good these witches didn't just come up with the notion you, of all people, are a druid. No, they had to have help. Let's see. Who hates you?" Sean asked.

"Everyone," Francis replied.

"Oi know that, ya dunce, but who hates you more than any other? Who knows you for the despicable wretch – who waters his beer and overcharges his customers to a nearly criminal degree – that you are?"

"Everyone?" Francis answered.

"Alright, who have you tossed out of your pub recently? Someone who might hold a grudge and want to do you a mischief," Sean said with frustration rising.

"At one time or another, everyone except Fr. Fahey," a dejected Francis Mulherin said and sadness scratched deep lines into his face.

"Think, Francis, ya nitwit," Sean commiserated. "Who is someone who you have tossed out of your pub and who trades in filthy lies?"

"I don't know. If I did, I would take a stick to the rascal," Francis said with iron in his voice.

"Well, right would be on your side if you gave him a good beatin'. Still, who would put the witches on you? Think," Sean instructed.

"I tell you, I don't know!" Francis shouted.

"Mulherin, you monumental eejit. Use that head of yours for something other than a hat rack. Think! Who brought the witches here to begin with?" Sean shouted.

"I tell you, I don't…," a sudden thought turned Mulherin's lips into a murderous snarl. "Cahill."

"Our mayor? You think that's possible? Oh, Oi am sure he would never do such a low, cowardly, vicious thing as that all because you threw him out of your establishment for not paying his bill and who vowed revenge on you and who has been slandering you all over the valley. Surely, not him. Oi'm shocked," Sean-the-Innocent said.

"Cahill," Francis said.

"Now, Francis, you mustn't do anything rash."

"Cahill."

"There will be no beating him with a good stout stick. Oi'm afraid Oi can't allow it, although Oi'm off duty Thursday. Why, that's tomorrow," Sean said with a sudden flash of recognition.

"Cahill…"

"Just because he said those things about your own sweet mother," Sean added.

"CAHILL!!" Francis Mulherin seethed and went looking for a good stout stick.

* * *

# CHAPTER TWELVE

Inspector Flannigan sat in a rocking chair before the turf fire in Julian's cottage. They had returned from another crime scene. Julian had a vision of the bomber this time, but it was skewed, indistinct. He could nearly see the man, but was never in a position to see his face or anything remotely identifiable.

"When we go to the scenes of these attacks, what are you looking for?" the inspector asked.

"I don't mean to be cryptic, but I'm looking for what is there and what isn't. I suppose you could say I am forming an impression of the person perpetrating these crimes," Julian said and snorted.

"Will you just listen to me," he said. "'These crimes'. That pretty much sanitizes the situation. I really must remember not to fool myself even for a moment. These crimes are murders. They are atrocities meant to terrorize innocent people.

"I'm sorry, inspector," Julian continued. "I get worked up about this. I also need to remember, as a professional, you have to remain detached or you can't do your job. Let's get back to your job.

"We've been through four sets of interviews with suspects," Julian said. "The only results were some minor criminals, a communist or two and an anarchist. Most don't have the smarts to tie their own shoes let alone pull off a string of bombings. The Gardaí don't have anything to go on yet?" Julian asked.

Inspector Flannigan answered, "Mr. Blessing, our forensics division and the bomb squad have been over the evidence. Every member of the force is beating the bushes and squeezing informants to see what we can get out of people.

"Our first thought, of course, was some Unionist faction or a dissident offshoot of the IRA and we beat that bush hard. It turned into a dead end. Unfortunately, we have only this lot of clods for now." His cell phone rang and the inspector said, "Just a moment", and stepped outside.

* * *

A well-dressed young man walked out the double doors and stepped into bright sunshine outside Keshk Café Restaurant. He hefted his briefcase and thought about the plate of falafel he had just enjoyed. The deep fried balls of ground chickpeas, tahini, garlic, onion and fresh coriander had been spiced with a light hand and served with still-warm pita bread.

He set a relaxed pace down Mespil Road, looking both ways before crossing Flemmings Place. He did the same at the Burlington Road crossing. It was a one-way street, but one can never be too careful.

He sighed and opened the door of 40 Mespil Road. It took him only moments to do what he had come for.

Nine minutes later as he approached Sussex Terrace, behind him, the head office of the Bank of Ireland at 40 Mespil Road shuddered for a millisecond before the interior was turned into a carnage-littered crime scene.

* * *

"Having any luck with your murder investigation?" pub keeper Mike O'Gavagan asked Sean Maher.

"Ach, it was just an accident. The lad probably just poisoned himself by mistake. That's what Oi think," Sean said before downing the last of his Guinness.

"How do you prove it one way or another?" Mike asked.

"Well, Oi need to start interviewing people. Witnesses, if Oi can find any, which Oi doubt. Lacking any of them, Oi have to find likely suspects," Sean answered.

"Sounds like thirsty work," Mike said and set another stout in front of Sean.

* * *

"Poor Edward," Lavonia Grayhawk said. "He seemed like a nice person. Not part of my coven, of course.

"Well, then whose coven is he part of? Everyone Oi've talked to tells a different story," Sean said and frustration turned his lips into an irritated snarl.

"Well, everyone is afraid to say anything," Lavonia said.

"Are you afraid?" Sean asked seeing a shimmer of hope.

"Of course not. She is like any other witch. Still, one can't be too careful. She has a charisma that attracts people. A number of my people have already applied to take Edward's place in her coven. Her popularity repels some too. Jealousy I suppose.

"The problem I see is she could be one of those people who trade on a person's spiritual nature in order to get money or power or whatever. I've heard she is actually nothing but a cult leader or con artist. Not that there is much difference. Then again, I've heard she is just a misunderstood white witch," Lavonia concluded.

"A white witch?" Sean asked. "Are there black witches? I think I know one of those."

"You're talking about Mrs. Hagan. I really don't think she is a witch at all. She just seems to be really eccentric and cranky," Lavonia said. "Anyway, I don't believe there are two different kinds of witches. Like everyone, sometimes you have a good day, sometimes you don't. Sometimes you're a white witch and sometimes you're not in a good place so ya get a little dark."

"Who is this person and where do Oi find her?" Sean asked.

Lavonia thought for a moment before taking a deep breath and saying, "No one I've talked to knows her real name. I've heard her called Lady Vanessa and the White Witch. She is the leader of the Solis Luna coven. They've made camp in the center of the woods east of the village.

"If you go see her, I wouldn't go alone, Mr. Maher," Lavonia said. "And don't mention my name, okay?"

"No offense, but no witch is going to best Sean Maher," Sean Maher said.

Lavonia rolled her eyes and foresaw dark possibilities.

\* \* \*

Inspector Flannigan said, "That was my chief superintendent. There has been an explosion in the city. They're still counting, but fifteen people are dead and a dozen are injured.

"I am to get back to Dublin. My chief is on his way here now and asks that you please make yourself available," Flannigan said.

Julian closed his eyes and nodded once.

✳ ✳ ✳

The clearing in the east woods was a bucolic painting of peace and harmony. At least Sean thought so.

"You are the White Witch and the leader of the Solis Luna coven, miss?" Sean asked and looked expectant.

An attractive, redheaded witch in a flowing pure white robe and red slippers stood at Sean's approach. Sensuous lips with a radiant smile and hooded blue gray eyes captivated Sean from the first.

"We are all white witches here. We practice our craft in the light and spurn the darkness. To your second question, yes, to the degree that we have a leader, that would be me," the White Witch said.

"Edward Biggins was a member of your group?" Sean asked. He smiled.

The White Witch went from a dazzling smile to a look of pure melancholy. "Yes, poor Edward was a part of our coven. He hadn't been with us long. He was new to the craft, but showed real potential. We will all miss him greatly," she said.

"Can you tell me what he was doing at the river?" Sean asked.

"I am afraid I cannot," the White Witch said.

"Well then, that takes care of my questions. Thank you for your time," Sean-the-Besotted said and produced a luminous smile of his own.

"Anytime I can be of service, do not hesitate to call on me," the White Witch said.

∗ ∗ ∗

"What do you mean she doesn't know anything?" Moira demanded. "How could she not?"

"Well, Oi asked her what she knew and she said she didn't know anything," Sean said.

"Nothing gets by you now does it," Moira said and acid dripped all over Sean Maher.

"Let's go see this witch who knows nothing," Moira said to Sean.

∗ ∗ ∗

Where Sean saw nothing but a pastoral scene of harmony, Moira saw nothing but discord, disagreement and a lot of dropped candy wrappers and Coke cans.

At the sound of Sean and Moira's approach to the White Witch's tent, she drew aside the flap looking resplendent in a diaphanous white robe.

"That I-don't-know-anything business may satisfy the curiosity of the Gardaí, but it doesn't do a thing for me!" Moira exploded.

"Let's start again, shall we? What is your name?" Moira demanded.

"Vanessa," the White Witch said.

"Not Lady Vanessa? I'm shocked. What is your last name?" Moira said.

"Does it matter?" the White Witch asked.

"It does to me because you're not delighted to share it with us," Moira said.

"Warden. Vanessa Warden, and yours?"

"I don't figure into this. Tell me about Edward Biggins?" Moira asked in her unique it-isn't-a-question manner.

"I don't know what there is to say. He was a faithful student who studied his craft. He was with us for a time and now he is dead. Is there anything else you would like to know?" the White Witch asked.

"Why do I have the feeling you are hiding more than a little something?" Moira said.

"I suspect you have a suspicious nature," the White Witch said pleasantly.

"The boy was poisoned," Moira said without expression.

"Oh my, that is distressing. I am sorry to hear it. Do you have any suspects?" the White Witch asked looking to Sean.

"Well…," Sean began.

"So far, he only has one suspect. You," Moira said.

"What makes me a suspect?" the White Witch asked.

"Odd that you would jump to the conclusion of murder first. Why not ask if he accidentally or intentionally poisoned himself?" Moira asked and a sneer cut her voice when she continued, "As to why you are a suspect, it is because I don't like you overly much and I think you know more than you're saying."

"I am sorry to hear that," the White Witch said.

"Maher, we are going. I have work to do," Moira said.

"Good day to you, milady. Good day Mr. Maher," the White Witch said.

*  *  *

"Mr. Blessing," Chief Superintendent Murphy began, "the head office of the Bank of Ireland was the site of an explosion at 11:42 this morning. A briefcase bomb containing a quantity of C4 explosive was placed beside a table. It left the bank interior a mass of wreckage and human remains. The death toll has risen to eighteen and is expected to go higher."

"With the bank's cameras, you have identified the bomber?" Julian asked as he walked along the headlands with Murphy.

"I would very much like to say that was the case. I would like to say the suspect was in custody. I would like to say I am retired and a rich man living in the Bahamas. What I can say, however, is there was a massive power surge a few moments before a man with a brief case entered the bank. All bank and all of the CCTV cameras in the area failed and remained blank until well after he was away.

"Mr. Blessing, at 11:39 this morning our dispatch center received a telephone call from a cell phone we have been unable to identify. The message was clear enough. The caller said, 'Julian Blessing 11:42 A.M.' The caller had a slight Irish accent. That is all we know.

"Your thoughts on this would be much appreciated," the chief superintendent concluded.

Julian Blessing stopped walking, looked out across the darkening Irish Sea, closed his eyes slowly and whispered one word. "Manning."

\* \* \*

Julian grew frustrated dodging or deflecting the balls of energy Finbar launched at him. "Whenever you get tired of doin' it the hard way, just let me know," Finbar said.

Julian held up his hand, closed his eyes and smiled as he opened them again. "And what would you be grinnin' at, boyo?" Finbar demanded before unleashing an attack.

The energy he transmitted traveled out ten feet and bounced back at him from a shield Julian had put in place. It was difficult to tell if the shock of the thwarted attack or the sting of returning energy enraged Finbar more.

"Well, it would seem somehow along the way a piece of knowledge attached itself to you," Finbar shouted. He knocked down Julian's wall and again he launched an attack only to have it turned back on him by another wall.

Furious he said, "You erected two barriers at once. Very clever, but did you think to put up three?"

Julian examined his fingernails and said, "Roll the dice and find out, old man." Julian unleashed a blistering attack with each charge hitting Finbar in the chest.

"The thing I like about erecting shields is that I can get at you from my side, but you can't get at me from yours. Maybe I'll just create a box around you and leave you there for a while," Julian said.

Julian turned and bent over to pick up his jacket from a nearby stump. Finbar attacked again only to encounter a third wall.

"You don't trust me!" Finbar shouted. "With your lack of trust you will not go far."

"Oh, but you're wrong," Julian said. "I trust you absolutely. I trust you to try every dirty trick you know. In that way you are like most people. I trust you enough to not trust you at all."

"Bridget, Moira and let's not forget that girl of yours would be ashamed at your lack of faith in humanity," Finbar said while he laughed and danced a little jig. "You've learned a lot from your book. Let's hope it's enough."

"Enough for Manning?" Julian asked.

"Aye and Clarke too. You won't likely run into one without the other," Finbar said as they started to walk back to the monastery. "Sooner or later, you will go after them or they will come looking for you. Either way, Manning won't be alone. That's the way of it, lad."

"They will come to me. You can take that to the bank," Julian said.

Both men fell into an introspective silence as they walked.

* * *

# Chapter Thirteen

"Maher, everything is wrong with that creature. Everything. You can bet your last Guinness on that. Since nothing is more sacred than that to you, you know how sure I am," Moira said.

"Now what? If she is involved, she will be on her guard," Sean said. "Thanks to you, Oi might add."

"Right you are, laddie. And she will start to cover her tracks. That is where you will catch her," Moira said.

"She still didn't act guilty," Sean said.

"No, she is too good for that, but I could feel her change when things became uncomfortable. She tried to hide it, but she would have to be far more talented to get around me," Moira said.

\* \* \*

Julian sat down in a stand of trees nearest the monastery. The weather was its usual wintertime gray with hints of white near the far horizon. Fog began to roll in off the Irish Sea bringing with it a slight drizzle.

It was a day that reflected Julian's mood. Quiet, a bit brooding and dark, it was a day perfect for reflection in general and self-examination in particular.

When first he was called to follow the path he was on, he had resisted. He tried to ignore and then denounce, show defiance and, in the end, beg to have his gift taken from him.

His teacher, Moira Hagan, had told him, "In our world, you can't believe some things and not others. There will be no picking and choosing for you. It is a path you are on, a road you must follow to the end."

'On, a road you must follow to the end.' He mouthed the words. The Jesuit Book had reiterated it.

Julian had seen the results of the darkness and the light in action. He had felt the powerful pull from each. He had watched as a sea of darkness washed away the lives of others.

He had no doubts. The light was slowly pulling out of an abyss, restoring his life, his soul, himself. That thought should have buoyed his thoughts and his mood, but it only made him melancholy.

"The light is all that exists. The rest is a false reality. The light pushes back the darkness, exposes it for what it is – illusion." He repeated the words from the Jesuit Book and he smiled a slight smile.

Patience was called for. Julian was not a patient man.

＊ ＊ ＊

"The White Witch is gone," Sean said as he approached Moira in her garden.

"Scampered has she? I'm not surprised. Let's you and me go have a look," Moira said.

They arrived in the clearing to a scene of chaos. Witches aplenty were arguing, crying or taking down their tents and packing their things.

Moira said, "There's her tent. Let's go have a look inside."

"We can't do that without a warrant," Sean said.

Moira held out her hand. Three tent poles snapped in half and the tent collapsed. A stiff, breeze arose and the tent blew away. "A warrant to search a forest clearing? Don't be daft. Here, help me root through her belongings."

The search revealed a wide array of charms, amulets, mirrors, witch paraphernalia and regalia, an overabundance of red shoes, white robes and one leather pouch of wolfsbane.

"Don't touch it, ya eejit," Moira said to Sean. "That stuff will snuff you out like a candle. Now, go get me an intelligent looking witch. It may take some time."

Sean returned a surprisingly short time later with a surprisingly bright looking witch. A reedy boy of twenty with thick glasses and a receding hairline bowed to Moira. "What can I do for you, milady?"

"Stop talking like that. I'm no lady as you will soon see unless you answer sharp. Now, where did your leader go?" Moira asked.

"No one knows. She disappeared during the night. We all hope nothing happened to her. Everyone is lost without her and many want to go home."

"I'm betting that's not the only thing lost," Moira said holding up an unlocked cash box. Empty.

\* \* \*

"How did that place turn into such a pig sty? First time Oi was there, it was neat and clean and everybody seemed happy. That Vanessa person must have been holding the place together," Sean said.

Moira stopped walking and said, "'Holding the place together.' I should have known. That's positively bright on your part."

Sean stopped and walked back to where Moira stood. "You're welcome, but how am Oi positively bright again?"

"Believe me, you being bright is as big a mystery to me as it is to you. Put it down to just random chance," Bridget said and Sean ground his teeth.

"You should have known what? You mean there is something you didn't know? Say it isn't so," Sean said.

"Don't make me smack you. I don't know why I didn't feel it sooner though. Everything was wrong with that woman. I should have known," Moira said her faced twisted in concentration.

\* \* \*

"What a surprise," the White Witch said.

Moira looked up to find the woman standing at the edge of the clearing near her tent.

Moira said, "Believe me, the surprise is all mine. I didn't expect to see you again, at least this side of a prison cell. Sorry about the tent. It fell down."

"A prison cell? Why ever would you say that?" the White Witch asked.

"Oh, I don't know. Mayhaps it is you being in possession of the poison that did in your Mr. Biggins. Maybe it is that you scampered with the accumulated wealth of your followers," Moira said.

A crowd of Solis Luna witches had gathered behind Moira and Sean. Muffled grumbling could be heard cascading throughout the followers as the White Witch stood serene and regal.

"What poison is that?" the White Witch asked.

"Wolfsbane. You had a leather bag full of the stuff," Sean said.

"Oh, you've been going through my things I see. No matter, I have nothing to hide. Although I am a trained herbalist, many of the members of the coven are not. Wolfsbane is a very dangerous herb, but young witches gather it during what I like to think of as their collecting stage.

"Although once thought of as a treatment for lycanthropy, that's the…"

"Werewolfism, yes, we know," Moira said.

"Yes, I thought you would," the White Witch said and Moira snorted.

"In any case, wolfsbane or other dangerous herbs have no place in this coven. So, when I learn someone has it, I confiscate it for everyone's protection whenever I find it. Speaking of which, in history, it has been sprinkled around farm animals to keep werewolves away. Just saying," the White Witch said.

"Wait a minute. Are you saying covens other than yours have this stuff?" Sean asked.

"That is entirely possible, even likely," the White Witch said.

"And as for making off with everyone's valuables?" Moira asked more pleasantly then her face let on.

"I knew I would be deep in the woods for the night. I took the coven's valuables with me for safe keeping," the White Witch said and looked at the remains of her tent. She opened a large leather bag and displayed money and jewelry.

"And you were alone?" Sean asked.

"In the forest one is never truly alone, but I had no human companions," the White Witch said.

"And what exactly were you doing in the woods?" Moira asked.

"You have no right to question Lady Vanessa!" an older witch in the crowd shouted. A general assent rippled through the coven.

Moira turned to stare down the crowd, but the White Witch held up a hand. At the gesture, the crowd fell silent.

In ringing majestic tones, the White Witch said, "These fine people are attempting to get to the bottom of our friend, Edward's death. Please allow them to speak."

"Do I need to ask the question again?" Moira asked with a sneer.

"Of course not. I went deeper into the woods to attune myself with the natural rhythm of life forces. Finding the creative center of the universe is an important part of our belief," the White Witch said.

With a smirk, Moira said, "Maher, we're going before we get covered in any more bilge water. We'll get no straight answers from this one today." Sean and Moira began their walk across the clearing and back to the village.

Moira stopped and turned. She projected the thought, *"Don't think I accept a word of what you're saying. You are guilty of something and I aim to find out what it is."*

The White Witch sent back her own thought. *"I await your pleasure, milady. Anything I can do to help you, I will do."*

*"Telepathic and you're able to project pretty pictures. Nice tricks both. Those, however, are your first mistakes. I look forward to many more,"* Moira thought.

The White Witch inclined her head and smiled a subdued, pinched-eyed smile.

* * *

"Finbar, why are you here?" Julian asked during his daily discussions.

"Because I'm not elsewhere?" Finbar answered with a chuckle.

"You could be a comedian. You would suck at it, of course, but it could happen. There are a lot of sucky comedians," Julian said.

"Why are you working with me? How did you get to be who you are? God knows you've quizzed me about that sort of thing often enough."

"Well, son, that is a tale. Not one worth telling or listening to, but I'll tell you because you asked nicely." The old man laughed again.

"You may have noticed, I am rather short in height. As I've proved with that ox Maher, I am rather tall in stature however. It wasn't always that way though. I was teased, mocked and beaten throughout me younger years. I'm sure you've noticed, children can be dreadful creatures, but adults can be worse. Far worse," Finbar said with a smile that harkened back to a painful time.

"One day, an old man came to the village. He talked with me parents, money changed hands and I was sent away with him as an apprentice. I would have been about eight or maybe ten. I really don't recall."

"We walked for several days and nights, but he never spoke to me even though I asked questions. Ultimately we arrived at a hut deep in a blackthorn forest. I was young and had never been out of the village. It seemed like a forest to me at the time anyway, although I discovered it really was quite tiny."

"The first words the man said to me are indelibly burned into my memory. He invited me to sit with him on the porch. 'You are special and we will make you more so,' he said. That's it. It was the first kindness I had ever been shown. I was devoted to the old man from that point forward."

"Like you, I was a quick study. I started early in life, so by the time I was a quarter your age, I was about a tenth as good as you are now. I was a quick little spark, but you are lightning, lad," Finbar said.

"The old man was patience personified, but insanely exacting. Like you, like Bridget for all that, if it wasn't perfect, it wasn't right. More than that, he refused to let me advance into different areas of the craft until I had first attained something like wisdom.

"During our time together, many of our sort came to visit. Some came to learn. Others came for healing. The broken, the bent, the tired, the curious – we saw to them and treated them all," Finbar said.

"In time, as my mentor aged and easily tired, I was left on me own to treat our patients. Aye, I tended to the local people too when we could and prayed over those we couldn't help. Occasionally, we would lose one of our own. There are relatively few of us so any loss is a great one.

"Sometimes, the damage was just too great. Sometimes the pressure of the mist and the light and the darkness, proved to be too much. Some we helped step down and return to a normal life. I can tell you that never ended well. Once you've seen both sides, you can't un-see it," Finbar said.

"And Bridget?" Julian asked.

"Ah Bridget, is it? Now there is a woman and a practitioner of an unequaled degree. I won't give you the details. First, they are none of your business. Second, if you want to know, ask her. She will box your ears of course, so there is that to consider before you ask.

"What I can tell you is she, her mentor and her teacher were caught in an ambush. She escaped while her companions fought the good fight to the end. She was badly injured inside and out. That is how she ended up on our doorstep.

"Like you, she was not one for half measures. An exercise went perfectly or it was begun again. She was her harshest critic. As she healed, she practiced. As she practiced, she grew in experience and wisdom, but she was never able to give up her need for revenge. Sound familiar?" Finbar asked.

"One day we returned from an especially taxing workout. We found the old man in his rocking chair on the porch of his cabin. He had a book in his lap and a last smile on his wrinkled and craggy face. Bridget and I buried him and she stayed with me through me own healing.

"In the end our mutual healing was done. The little hut had been my teacher's, not mine. I packed up his books and went off looking for a spot of me own. I found it a distance from your home of Cappel Vale in a place called the Near Woods. Since it is many leagues from anywhere, what the woods are near, I've never discovered.

"Several years passed. I was called on many times to tend to those like us who were in need. Built a fair reputation as a healer of broken souls while I was at it too. But one day, Bridget came to visit. She needed my help, so off we went to hunt the darkness that had ended the lives of her mentor and her teacher.

"We found what we were looking for and made short work of the venture. She then returned to her life, and I to mine, although we've remained close through the years. There have been times when I've needed her second sight and times when she needed me," Finbar said and took out his pipe.

"So, she is the one who called you to deal with me?" Julian asked.

Finbar went through his ritual of packing and lighting his pipe. "Julian, old son, everyone called to have me take a go at you. Bridget was the second to call. One of these days you will wake up and discover you have more friends, associates and admirers than you could imagine. You may also discover how many enemies you have."

"Who called you first?" Julian asked, closed his eyes and waited for the answer he knew would come.

"Your friend from Rome, Fr. Marek Soski." Finbar's voice was as soft as a whisper.

"You knew him?" Julian asked.

"It was my very great privilege. He came to me after he was injured a long time ago. It took nearly a year, but he healed and returned to the Vatican. Sadly, there were thoughts of revenge in his heart as well. Seems to be a lot of that going around. Still, he was a good man," Finbar answered.

"Yes, he was a good man. Far better than I will ever be and I helped kill him," Julian said as tears brimmed his pale gray eyes.

"Well, son, that's progress."

"What?" Julian was incredulous.

"A month ago you said you killed him yourself. Now you only helped. That is progress."

"Drop this Finbar while you still can," Julian said.

"Why? Separate your need for revenge from the anger you feel for yourself. You've made a start at that, but give Fr. Soski's life meaning. Understand he is a part of you. As long as you remember, he will be with you," Finbar said.

"One day you will be able to forgive yourself, but understand and give him credit. The good father had choices to make and he made them willingly as did you," Finbar said.

# Chapter Fourteen

"Ailís, darlin'," Fr. Fahey said as he caught up with the doctor walking up the main street in Cappel Vale. "Seems like it's been dog years since Oi've seen you."

"What kind of talk is that father? Timothy and I were in church on Sunday," Ailís said and smiled.

"Ach, you know what Oi mean. How go things with you?" the priest asked.

"Hectic with my patients and Timothy keeps me busy. I don't have time for much else. I do owe you dinner though. I've not forgotten," she said.

The priest stopped and turned to face the doctor. They had not yet entered the center of the village. "Oi didn't ask if you were keeping busy. Yours is a soul in torment. Tell me what Oi can do," he stated.

They started walking again. "Father, I truly wish there was something you or anyone could do. What has me sick at heart is completely out of my control. There is nothing for it, but to wait. I'm not the waiting kind," Ailís said.

"We are talking about Julian," the priest said. "Oi don't know the details and don't need to know them. He is off licking his wounds Oi suspect. An all too common response to severe trauma. Julian is a strong fella, smart and good looking too, eh?" he nudged her to get a smile.

"Yes he is all of that and so much more, father. You remember. Kind and giving and tender beyond belief. He would do anything for a person and never even expect a thank you. He is the partner I've always wanted. I love him so much," the doctor said.

"Oi realize this is hard for you. Patience is a virtue they say, but it is one you do not possess. You are being asked to do that thing that is the most difficult for you, watch and wait. You must build up your reserves. You must be ready," Fr. Fahey said.

"Father, everyone tells me that. All I want to do is take him in my arms and tell him everything will be alright. I realize I'm being foolish wanting what I can't have," Ailís said.

"My girl, isn't it you and Oi who make our living caring for others? It is your nature to want to heal. Why should it come as a surprise you would want to mend the man you love?"

"Thank you for listening, father. Your kindness and your caring are appreciated," Ailís said and smiled a sad smile and the priest patted her arm.

* * *

Ailís sat on the railing of her front porch after her last patient left. She pulled her sweater close around her and smiled at the memory of the first time Julian wrapped her in his arms.

She could feel him warm and strong against her. She could smell his freshly washed skin. She could feel his hands move slowly over her. She had mended his battered and bruised body and healed his heart after she had broken it.

"Through my own stupidity, I nearly lost you. Never again," she whispered.

She smiled as she remembered when he entered the village and her life. He wasn't there one moment and the next he was and her world was upside down. Never had she been drawn to a person so quickly. She thought about him standing in the police station that Sean Maher occupied now.

There Julian was, tall, handsome, frighteningly intense and very much lost and alone. She watched as he began to rebuild himself. Witnessed him becoming a fixture in the village. Looked on with concern as he and Moira spent time together and he changed into a more powerful version of himself.

"I tried to be angry with you. Tried to dismiss you. Tried to ignore you. Tried to put you out of my mind. In the end I had to admit to myself how much I loved you. You will never know how much, Julian Blessing, but I'll not let you forget it when you return. If you return," she said to no one in particular.

* * *

"Dublin is still undergoing bombings?" Finbar asked.

"They have spread to Wexford and Cork. All with my name attached to them," Julian said as the two men walked along a craggy outcrop. The monastery could be seen in the distance. Its tall, narrow chapel spire stark against the afternoon sky.

"Your plan hasn't changed?" Finbar asked.

"As we've agreed, reacting won't accomplish anything. As you've said, Manning has another purpose for the bombings other than to draw me out. They will continue no matter what I do and people will continue to die. I lose if I go for him.

"Finbar, in Rome, Manning had Fr. Soski and me chasing our tails. We were manipulated from start to finish and never saw it. We played his game on his terms and he had the home field advantage. This time it will be different.

"He is a man with many unique talents. He was able to install and maintain a shield not only around his thoughts and actions, but the entire operation. He is doing the same now much to Bridget's consternation," Julian said and pulled his jacket close around him.

"He has a lot to account for, Finbar," Julian said, "and I mean to make that happen right here. If I am going to win, and contain the loss of life, he must come here."

"And if you don't win?" Finbar asked.

"That's why I need every advantage I can get. If I lose, we all lose," Julian said. "Why do you keep asking?"

"Because I need to know you are committed. I need you to understand you may die because of the choices you are making," Finbar answered.

"Believe me, I know what is at stake."

\* \* \*

"Mrs. Hagan," Timothy Dwyer shouted while banging on the door to Moira's cottage.

Moira opened the door and cast a malevolent eye on the boy. "There is some reason you are carrying on?" she asked.

"You have to come quick. They found another body in the river," Timothy said.

"Your mother and Mr. Maher?" Moira asked.

"They're already there. Isn't this exciting? Two bodies in as many days." Timothy was ecstatic and it showed in the wide-eyed enthusiasm that animated his face.

* * *

"Mrs. Bridget Bragonier," the deputy commissioner of the Garda Síochána said to Superintendent Murphy.

"I know the name, but I've never met the lady," Murphy said.

"Count yourself lucky. She is the soul of wit and charm, is connected and formidable. And, I'll add, terrifying beyond reason," Deputy Commissioner Kelly said.

"All that," Murphy said.

"All that and more. I don't want to know how much more. They say she has the Dà Shealladh," Kelly said.

"The second sight, sir? I knew someone once who was said to have it. He put my teeth on edge when I was introduced. I avoided his company after that," Murphy said.

"So, it's secrets you have?" Kelly needled.

"We all do, sir," Murphy said.

"They say Mrs. Bragonier's talents are not limited to the sight. There are others who are as talented as she as well. Your group is working with one such now. I don't need to tell you, he comes to us by way of no less than the Taoiseach," Kelly said.

"Julian Blessing has the sight?" Murphy asked and his eyes went wide.

"I have no idea what he has or hasn't, but I want to know and quickly," Kelly said, then continued. "Murphy, there is a darker side to all of this. There is a man named Manning. He managed to murder a slew of people, three of whom were ours. I have been advised he is somehow like Blessing and the Bragonier woman. I want Manning brought in and this Blessing may be able to assist."

"You have a man working closely with Blessing on the bombings?" Kelly asked.

"I do. Inspector Flannigan. Bright young chap. New to the job, but up to the task," Murphy answered.

"Good. I want that man to know everything there is to know about Blessing in particular and these people in general. Their existence has been whispered about for generations, but we don't have any specifics. I want specifics," Kelly said.

"More than that, I want Mrs. Bragonier interviewed to see what she does and doesn't know about this Manning and whatever other information we can gather on Blessing and the bombings."

"And the Taoiseach's other troubles? The leaks in his government?" Murphy asked.

"The Taoiseach's leaks are the Taoiseach's problem. I'm interested in stopping the loss of life this bomber has visited on us and I want to know about those people," Kelly stated and brooked no further discussion.

\* \* \*

"Sir, Inspector Flannigan to see you," the superintendent's secretary said over the intercom.

"Send him in," Superintendent Murphy said.

"Sir, may I have a word?" Inspector Flannigan asked as he stuck his head around the door to his superintendent's office.

"I was about to start looking for you, Flannigan. I've a meeting to attend in a few minutes, but I wanted a word with you. You go first," Superintendent Murphy said.

Flannigan entered, but wasn't invited to sit. "Sir, Mr. Blessing and I have interviewed quite a number of suspects and have visited many of the bombing crime scenes. I don't know how to put this sir, but is there something I should know about him?" Flannigan asked.

"Ah, you've noticed. I've been advised this Blessing character is, well, different," Murphy said.

"Different, sir – the man is some sort of human lie detector. I take him a suspect, and I swear to you, sir, Blessing looks at the bloke and the man starts quivering and spilling his guts. These are hard case criminals of long standing, aye and anarchists and the like. That and his eyes look right into you. The man is frightening. God, this sounds stupid," Flannigan said and looked pained that he didn't have the right words. "And it gets worse. We look at crime scenes and he is able to supply all sorts of disjointed information. It is as though Blessing is there, but can't see clearly," Flannigan said in frustration. "I've not the words to describe this."

"Flannigan." The superintendent sat back in his chair, crossed his arms and said, "I don't have any answers for you, beyond this; Blessing is a special case. Handle him with great care, learn as much as you can about him and get as close to him as possible. You're the inspector. Figure it out, but I want you to become the resident expert on Julian Blessing and the rest," the superintendent said.

"Rest, sir? There are more like him? Sweet Jasus," the inspector said. "Sorry, sir."

"Based on what I have been told, 'Sweet Jasus,' is a sentiment I share, son," the older man said.

"I have another assignment for you. Here is the name and address of a woman here in Dublin. I want you to go interview her," Murphy said.

"Interview her about what? Does she know something about the bombings?" Flannigan asked.

"Lad, I don't know what she knows and what she doesn't know. It is suspected she has the sight. I want to know what she can tell us about Blessing and a man named Manning and if she knows anything about these damned bombings.

"I wouldn't send you into this blindly, but it is little else I can tell you. I can say only what I've been told. Firstly, she is like Blessing. Second, prepare to be terrified." The Superintendent gathered a few file folders from his desk and stood. The interview was over.

* * *

"Let me guess," Moira said. "Another witch?"

"Since there is a superabundance of them the odds would be on your side," Ailís said. "Drowning from what I can tell."

"More wolfsbane?" Moira asked as she knelt to examine the body. A blond woman in her mid-twenties was laid out respectfully at the river's edge. Her cloak and robe were unadorned, but of good quality. A rope was tied around her waist.

"Not poison this time. Suicide," Moira said and her tone was without inflection. She looked sad and touched the young woman's cold wet cheek.

"What makes you say that?" Sean asked.

"The rope. The poor dear probably tied the other end to a rock, carried it to the deep part of the river and the rest is easy enough to see. Chances are the rope came untied or we might not have found her for a while."

"You should be a detective," Sean said.

"You should be beaten," Moira said.

"Enough you two. Sean, same as last time. Clear these people out and call for the medical examiner to take her away. Moira is probably right though," Ailís said. "Find out the girl's name and what group she was with."

"Already done. At least the name and all. She was Ronda Lipmann." Sean looked at Moira. "She was with the Solis Luna coven."

\* \* \*

Ailís' life was a blur of busy days and sleepless nights. It was winter and farmers had the time to be sick. She treated them all from broken arms to those who needed a kind word from a friend.

At night, her nightmares would appear.

She had flown to Rome to surprise Julian. Being with him in the eternal city was nothing but a luxury. She went to pick up a package for him, but managed to get kidnapped instead.

Under the pretext of Julian being injured, she had willingly joined her kidnappers. Bundled into a car, she was drugged and woke up in a small, dank apartment. For a week she endured absolute silence. Without human contact she began to imagine. All the what-if's merged into nightmares of violence and death.

Freed by Fr. Soski, she managed to escape unharmed physically, but Julian hadn't been so lucky. He suffered serious physical injuries, but his deepest wounds, the wounds that left her in anguish were mental and emotional.

Her Julian was lost to her. For now.

\* \* \*

"Timothy," Ailís Dwyer said. "You got into another fight at school. The sisters are very cross with you and I'm not a'tall pleased with your behavior."

"It wasn't my fault. Someone made fun of me mate, Brendan," Timothy began before his mother interrupted.

"My friend Brendan – if you please," Ailís said in her sternest voice.

Timothy began again. "I couldn't let that pass, so I got into a fight and lost. Again. I always lose. I'm too small," Timothy Dwyer said.

"Brendan Maher can more than take care of himself," Ailís said.

"You know Brendan is slow. Well, Jimmy Doyle said Brendan was a freak and a retard. What else could I do?" Timothy pleaded.

"Yes, Brendan is challenged. What Jimmy said was cruel and stupid and I will take it up with the boy's father," Ailís began.

"Mamma, no! You can't do that or I would be in more fights. Don't you see, if you talk to Jimmy's da, I'll take no end of ribbing for having me mother…"

"My mother," Ailís corrected. "And it is Jimmy's father, not Jimmy's da. I am not sending you to school to be a hooligan," Ailís said.

"For having my mother fight for me. We can't have that now, can we?" Timothy asked.

Ailís smiled a slight smile and shook her head at the unassailable logic of a twelve-year-old.

* * *

Ailís came to his mind. He could see her clearly, but could not feel her. He could see Timothy, a boy he had come to love with an intensity that startled him.

Ailís. Timothy. They were his light in a very dark place.

He remembered meeting them both and floated in the warm feelings those memories engendered. The village of Cappel Vale and its many odd citizens, the love he had for Ailís and Timothy – they were his home and his life.

"If I lose, I lose everything," Julian whispered.

* * *

Moira and Sean approached the White Witch as she stood at the center of her coven in their clearing.

"Ronda Lipmann is dead," Moira said.

"Oh, very subtle that is," Sean said under his breath.

"That's terrible," the White Witch said and lost color in her cheeks. The rest of the coven became noisy and restless. "When did this happen?" she asked.

"That is impossible to determine, but it was recent," Sean said.

"The how of it doesn't seem to matter to you. Could it be because you already know?" Moira asked.

"Of course I don't know. How could I? I see no reason to be morbid about it though. The poor girl is dead."

"Miss Warden, you seem to be losing a lot of followers. Is there a connection between Miss Lipmann and Mr. Biggins?" Sean asked.

"None that I know of," the White Witch said and a murmur rolled through the coven. "If any of you knows anything, come forward now. If you don't want to speak in front of the group, see Mr. Maher in private," the White Witch said.

"If you will excuse us, we need to mourn Ronda and celebrate her life as we did Edward's. This is our way," a rattled White Witch said.

\* \* \*

# CHAPTER FIFTEEN

John Clarke stopped a young man walking down Grafton Street. "In a moment," Clarke said, "I am going to be gone and you are going to be dead."

"Pardon me? I'm afraid I don't know what you are talking about," the well-dressed young man said.

Clarke projected his thought. *"Oh but you do. You see, I am going to walk away and you will have a live satchel bomb just full of explosives in your hands."* Clarke smiled and looked down at a briefcase in the young man's hand. *"You see, old boy, I need only delay you for another minute and you will be so much meat on a corner's table alongside so many others."*

"After you have completed your task, present yourself at this address." Clarke handed over a folded piece of heavy note paper and continued on his way His smile communicated it all. The pleasure taken in murder and destruction, even vicariously, was a wonderful feeling.

The young man hurried into the Brown Thomas department store on Grafton Street. He proceeded to the espresso bar on the third floor and forced himself to slow his pace to avoid attracting attention.

Setting his briefcase down near the bar, he turned and made his way back downstairs and out of the building. He walked across the street a little faster than he intended to. He entered Marks & Spencer, rounded the main staircase and made it through a side door onto Duke Street before the explosion rocked a half block of Grafton Street and threw a passing taxi through the front window of the nearby McDonald's.

Clarke had been right. The young man had nearly been caught holding the bag.

\* \* \*

Julian and Inspector Flannigan walked without particular purpose down Grafton Street.

"Mr. Blessing, how are you able to do what you do?" the inspector asked.

Julian thought for a long several moments before saying, "Inspector, it is difficult to explain. I've accepted a reality very different from your own, although I understand your reality all too clearly."

"I'm afraid I asked the wrong question. For example, you seem to know things you have no reason to know. How is that done?" the inspector asked and his forehead wrinkled in concentration.

"I would like to be able to answer your question, but the fact is, I simply know. You see I read people, not their thoughts but their emotions. From that, I've been lucky enough to accurately extrapolate. It appears I know things I shouldn't, but in fact mine are just educated guesses really.

"For instance, that young fella hurrying across the street toward Marks and Spenser…shit!" Julian grabbed the inspector and pushed him into a doorway. A second later, the upper stories of Brown Thomas department store erupted and rained down masonry, window glass and splintered woodwork.

"Go! Run!" Julian shouted at the inspector. "Down that street. Your bomber is the only one not in a hurry to get away from here!"

Jumping over debris and moving through glass shards, Inspector Flannigan did as instructed.

He ran.

\* \* \*

"Damn and hell! Nothing," Flannigan wheezed as he tried to catch his breath. "I saw him round a corner, but by the time I reached it, he was gone. Young is all I know. Early thirties maybe, but I couldn't swear to it."

Julian had pulled several people from the rubble. His shirt and jacket were covered in dirt and blood. In the distance, emergency service vehicles could be heard approaching. He sat on the curb and looked into the sweat-soaked face of Inspector Flannigan.

"Always the innocent suffer," Julian whispered. "Why?"

"Because it is the way it has always been," Flannigan said in sympathy.

\*\*\*107

"Julian, lad, you look like a man about to explode. What ails ya?" Finbar said.

"Manning's death toll for these bombings has crossed fifty. I've no choice but to hunt him down and stop this slaughter if I can," Julian answered.

"In doing that you would be making a very serious mistake," Finbar said and his tone of voice made Julian take notice.

The old man loaded his pipe, but didn't light it. "Listen, lad, I understand you want to bring this to an end. What you need to understand is a man like Manning doesn't do anything without having several goals in mind. He has personalized this by attaching your name to the bombings. Still, you have to know, you are an event, but not the main event.

"No, the bombings are meant to accomplish another goal," Finbar said. "Work on this from another direction.

"You know Manning and Clarke are not going to ruin their manicures by setting these bombs. One or more others are involved. They may be willing participants, but again they may not be. In any case, you already know who is behind the bombings. Isn't it time to work out who the bomber is?" Finbar asked.

"Listen to me, Julian," Finbar said. "I know you want to stop this. I do too, but if Manning and Clarke draw you out, they win. As you've pointed out yourself, you'll fight on their turf, on their terms and they will set the rules. That being the case, you will surely lose and aside from one more death, nothing will be accomplished.

"I know it's hard, but stay the course you've set and maintained thus far. Make them come to you," Finbar said.

\* \* \*

"Mr. Maher?" Two witches presented themselves at the police station. The milky sun had set and shadows slowly engulfed the village of Cappel Vale.

"Don't stand around out there. Come in," Sean called out.

"We are from the Solis Luna coven and we have some information for you," one witch said.

"First of all, tell me your names," Sean said with a kindly expression.

"I am Pearl and this is Garret. You don't need our last names, do you?"

Pearl was a middle aged woman with wispy blond hair and a hopeful expression. Her partner was a skinny boy in his early twenties with too much hair for Sean's taste, bad skin and a sulky disposition.

"For now, Pearl, no Oi don't. If what you have for me is important to my case, Oi will need them though," Sean said.

"I guess that's alright," Garret grumbled.

"We were tasked with packing up Ronda's things. Garret picked up her book of shadows and this fell out." Pearl handed over three pages of notebook paper. Tight cursive handwriting took up every inch of each page.

Sean pushed back in his chair, read the first few lines and said, "Why don't you two take a seat by the fire? This may take some time. Oi will have questions when Oi'm done reading, but Oi doubt there will be many," Sean said and let out a noisy breath.

Sean read and reread the pages. They told a story that was as old as human existence, but still heartbreaking in the telling.

"What is a book of shadows?" Sean asked when he was done reading.

"It is a sort of notebook where a witch records the various spells he or she casts and the results. It is a sort of journal where thoughts and feelings are set down, too. Like a diary, it is a very private and personal thing," Garret said.

"Do you have this book with you?" Sean asked.

Pearl reached into a woven bag and withdrew a green, leather bound volume with an embossed pentagram on the front cover. She handed it to Sean.

With some reverence, he took it into his large gnarled hands. Leafing through a few pages, he held the book up against separate note pages. The writing was the same or close enough that it couldn't have been written by someone else.

"Oi take it you have read this note?" Sean asked.

"We have, sir," Pearl said with tears brimming her eyes.

"Have you shared it with anyone, and Oi mean anyone, including your leader?" Sean asked.

"Of course we told Lady Vanessa, but she said to bring it to you right away," Garret said.

"You completed your task for poor Ronda and that is all you need tell anyone who asks. Do you understand?" Sean said.

The two witches looked at each other and nodded.

"It is procedure and not because Oi don't trust you, but please give me your passports. Oi will hold them until it is time for you to leave Ireland or when my investigation is completed," the big man said. "Ronda's book of shadows you can leave with me. You have my word, no one will disturb it and Oi will return it to you as soon as possible."

\* \* \*

"You can still walk away, Julian," Finbar whispered. The two men sat before the turf fire drinking too much porter and thinking dark thoughts.

"You know I can't," Julian mumbled drunkenly. "I thought about it. I've tried. Mostly, I've tried to make any of my decisions make sense. I am giving up everything in pursuit of something that well could kill me. The problem is, I can't let go of my friends, or they of me, until Manning is stopped," Julian said.

The fire popped. A few embers caught, flared and died. The air in Julian's cottage was thick with the smell from the peat fire. The aroma of rich, damp soil, newly cut hay and wildflower heather permeated everything.

"It isn't that I don't understand, lad, I do," Finbar said and hic-coughed. "The real problem though is, if you lose, your death means nothing, will solve nothing. I just want to make sure you have come to grips with that," Finbar said.

"I well could lose, but there is a chance I could win," Julian said in a drowsy whisper. "It is a chance I have to take. I couldn't live with myself if I didn't and many others might not have to die if I follow this to the end."

\* \* \*

"Quite a tale, eh?" Sean said when Moira had read the letter in silence.

"Tragic and one that has been told too many times before," Moira said with sadness touching her eyes.

"Let's see if Oi have it right," Sean said. "Edward was smitten with the Warden woman. A lusty one is that and she is a fine lookin' lass to boot. I can see how that is likely."

Moira punched his arm and said simply, "Pig."

"So, in order to impress the winsome Miss Warden, he mucks about with wolfsbane. Sadly, his experiment goes sideways and he ends up dead," Sean said as he stared into the peat fire.

"Still more sadly, Miss Ronda is in love with Edward. He doesn't know she exists since he is blinded by his lust for their leader," Sean said with a sad smile. "Poor Ronda is heartbroken at the death of her love, so she ends her pain in the river. Something very Irish about that really," Sean concluded.

"You've nearly got it, Sean me boy. That Warden creature is innocent in the deaths of Edward and Ronda it would seem. However, she isn't innocent. On that I will place money. Let's say five Euros?" Moira said.

"What else do you want, Moira?" Sean said. "The woman had nothing to do with these deaths."

"Well, then boyo, you trundle out there and give her the good news. Oh, and get your fiver ready." Moira said.

\* \* \*

"This is an unmitigated bust," Julian said with frustration cutting deeply into his face. He bunched his fists in annoyance at his inability to throw up a wall strong enough to withstand a full-on assault.

"Well," Finbar said, "I wouldn't say it is unmitigated. You're just an eejit. That would seem to be mitigation enough, eh?"

"Why am I an idiot – this time?" Julian asked.

"Well, son, you keep falling back on the notion this is all about you willing your defenses into existence. To make it worse you are also trying to strengthen and maintain them on your own," Finbar said. "Let's get this straight. You will lose your life if you continue as you are.

"You must learn to pull energy from every source and I do mean every source. Draw on the strength that is all around you," Finbar said. "Have you learned nothing? Now, get over there and we'll try again and we'll keep trying until you stop being an eejit."

"I don't know that we have enough time for that," Julian said.

"Poor you. Leave off with your whining and quit your dawdling. We have work to do and I don't have the time or the patience to coddle you. Ya eejit!" Finbar barked.

\* \* \*

"Here's your filthy money," Sean said as he handed over a crisp, gray five Euro note. "The White Witch scampered off and, no doubt about it, this time for good.

"The cash box is gone as are those white robes she wears," Sean said and snarled. "She left her little group out there standing in their clearing like a band of sheep. Poor creatures don't know what to do."

"How about the red slippers? I rather fancied those," Moira said.

"Gone," Sean said.

"Sad," Moira murmured. "Oh well, you should probably get a hold of whoever you get a hold of and tell 'em to watch the airports. It is only a precaution. I doubt they'll catch her, although I dare say caught she will be. Mark my words, she will surface again."

"They won't catch her, but she will be caught? What does that mean, if you don't mind my asking," Sean said and looked concerned. "I don't want you doing anything foolish."

"Never you mind about my foolishness, boyo. Right now, I'm going to hunt up that Lavonia Grayhawk person. Doubtless, she will incorporate Solis Luna's lost lambs into her group until they can sort things out," Moira said and gathered her shawl around her. "After that, I have something to attend to." Moira's smirk was nearly audible and carried a murmur of purest satisfaction.

✳ ✳ ✳

"Big Jimmy Kennedy, come in and speak to me, son," Sean said as he sat in the police station later in the day.

Kennedy was a large man with a short fuse. He was a farmer who grew up on his family's land and seldom came into the village.

"A herd of people, witches they said, showed up at me farm this morning. Oi hit one of 'em," Kennedy said.

"Hard?" Sean asked and winced. Any hit from Big Jimmy Kennedy would hurt.

"Oi didn't think so, but the lad thought he should go see the doctor anyway," Kennedy said.

"Oi'll look into it and smother any police report the lad tries to make against you," Sean said. "Anything else?"

"Why did they show up on me property?" Kennedy asked. "They said they had been sent to see me, but wouldn't tell me who sent 'em even after Oi hit another of 'em."

"Jimmy, you must stop hitting people," Sean said. "Mayhaps there are some who thought to pull a mischief on you."

"Don't be daft, Maher. Everyone knows better than that," Kennedy said.

"Could it be someone has a grievance against you?" Sean asked and looked expectant.

"It wouldn't be another farmer. We are all busy and haven't time for playing silly buggers," Kennedy said.

"You were in the village a week ago. Oi saw you meself," Sean said.

"Aye, Oi came in to pick up supplies."

"Well, Oi understand you did some little damage at O'Gavagan's pub," Sean remarked.

"Why 'twasn't nothing. Wasn't it that worthless Tom Walsh did most of the destruction?" Kennedy said.

"Aye, but who is it who threw you out, unjustly as it turns out?" Sean asked.

Kennedy thought for a moment and it was painful to see the cogs in his head moving. "Why, it was that even-more-worthless O'Gavagan," Kennedy growled.

"No, is that true?" Sean asked in all feigned innocence. "Surely, only a rascal, aye and a scoundrel would do such a thing to a fine man like your good self," Sean said.

Big Jimmy Kennedy went away with a flea in his ear, murder in his heart and O'Gavagan in his sights.

\* \* \*

"It's late for you to be out prowling the woods, isn't it, doctor?" Julian asked.

Startled by Julian's sudden appearance, Doctor Mahoney said, "I looked for you at your cottage. Since you weren't there and Finbar hadn't seen you, well, I knew you would be out here somewhere. I wanted to talk to you."

"About?" Julian asked as the two men walked toward the tree line facing the monastery. "Let's sit here." He indicated a fallen tree.

"Well, it is something I've wondered about since I came here. I've had scores of patients and have put my questions to each. All I get are cagey answers that don't answer anything," the doctor said.

"Well, ask your questions and I'll see if I can be less cagey," Julian said.

"I know each of you has a different set of skills. Some of those I know are adept at telepathy and telekinesis. A very few are clairvoyant. You seem to have that lot and psychoscopy as well. Although I've not seen you burn anything down, I suspect pyrokinesis and remote viewing are lurking in there somewhere," the doctor said.

"The question is an easy one, but one you lot wiggle out of each and every time. How? How do you do what you do? Where does the power come from?" the doctor asked.

"That only seems like a simple question. The truth is, I doubt there is anyone who can answer it," Julian said. "I'll give it a try, but don't be surprised if you go away with more questions than answers."

"You giving it a go would be surprise enough. The lot of you are notoriously tight lipped," the doctor said with the moonlight glinting off his glasses.

"Each of us is imbued with the ability to make choices. Nothing shocking there, but what if all of your choices were based on a false premise? Dark is dark and light is light. Simple, unless I convince you dark is light. Once you swallow that, what are your choices worth?" Julian asked.

"What we do is appeal to a truer sense of reality, a reality where everything is possible. Now, no one I've heard of has achieved that state, but with that true reality, it is possible. In your benighted world, it isn't that it isn't possible, it isn't even conceivable. True is false and false is true. Make your choices on that basis and you can see the outcome," Julian said and looked up at the moon as clouds scudded across its face.

"But you people harness tremendous amounts of power. I've seen it with my own eyes. Where does that come from?" the doctor asked.

"It can come from two sources. There is personal power, the kind that comes from within. This is a lowest common denominator because, although everyone has it, it is limited. By appealing to the energy that inhabits everything, one is limited only by one's ability to act as a conduit for that energy," Julian said.

"I don't believe it is that simple. You are having me on like all the rest," the doctor said.

"Have it your own way, doctor, but it is that simple and that complex. Humanity swallowed a lie a very long time ago and there are those who want to keep us on that diet of deceit.

"You believe the lie, believe that humanity is limited, doctor," Julian said. "Still, you have seen demonstrations that the lie is, in fact, a lie. You have seen it with your own eyes as you say and still, you can't trust yourself enough to know you have seen a different reality in action."

\* \* \*

# Chapter Sixteen

"A boil you say?" Sean asked. "And where is it located?"

"Indeed and, Sean Maher, it is none of your business where it is," Pat Sullivan said.

"And you say the crazy Hackett sisters gave you a poultice?" Sean asked.

"That they did," Sullivan said. "And whatever it was they gave me not only didn't work, it smelled to high heaven and me boil got bigger to boot."

"You don't suppose they gave you the wrong concoction on purpose, do you?" Sean said. "Oi mean, after all, it is no secret you're not well liked. They might have had it in for you."

"I'm not liked because Oi am prosperous. Is that my fault?" Sullivan said. "You don't suppose those batty sisters gave me the wrong poultice out of spite or envy, do you?"

"That's what Oi asked you, but Oi'm sure that's not the case. Perhaps you should go discuss the problem with them. Oi mean, they did give you a poultice that not only didn't work, but actually made the thing huge. Speaking of which, Oi noticed you are sitting a bit gingerly," Sean said.

"How Oi'm sitting is none of your business either. Oi'm going to go over their straight away and give them a good talking to!" Sullivan declared, whereupon he took his leave of Sean Maher and went hunting Hacketts.

\* \* \*

"Moira, something is very wrong. In the last few days, I've treated Mike O'Gavagan, Francis Mulherin, Jim Kennedy and Pat Sullivan. Tom Cahill I saw three times. You were the cause of two of Tom's visits, so I don't know whether to count those or not," Dr. Ailís Dwyer said.

The women were sitting in Moira Hagan's garden enjoying the unseasonably warm sunshine. Moira said, "Well, I've treated as many or more, all with cuts and bruises and lookin' the worse for wear. Even some of the visiting witches have taken their lumps."

"I can tell you, the Hackett sisters gave Pat Sullivan a thorough going over," Ailís said. "I don't know what possessed him to cross them. Apparently, they took their umbrellas to him. I don't see many umbrella-related injuries. I can tell you they are vicious."

"The Hacketts can be vicious. You know darlin', there is something passing strange," Moira said.

"What's that?" Ailís asked.

"We know who we've treated, and it is a lengthy list. The shorter list by far is who we haven't seen for various injuries."

"So short that it is suspicious to be sure," Ailís noted.

"That priest and the nuns are exempt of course," Moira said. "You and me, but no one is that daft as to bother us."

Ailís stood and growled, spilling a lap full of greens.

Moira's eyes narrowed.

Both women had an inkling and the inklings of women never bode well for anyone.

\* \* \*

Ailís stood in the open doorway of the police station. The weak sunlight stood behind her giving off an effective halo.

"A number of citizens have recently been injured. Quite a number actually. Nearly everyone really. What do you know about that?" Ailís asked. She had no plan of leaving without a confession. It was a police station after all, as good a place for confessions as a church.

"Doctor darlin'," Sean said, "in truth, Oi don't know what to tell you. It is as great a mystery to me as it is to you."

"You expect me to believe that?"

"'Tis the truth," Sean declared.

"The truth is it? This epidemic of dust ups came in two waves that can be distinctly identified. First, all your known enemies followed by everybody else. Still don't know anything about it?" Ailís asked in her sweetest voice.

"Beyond that, you don't happen to know who has been setting the visiting witches onto people, do you?" Ailís asked in her not-so-sweet voice.

"Oi really couldn't say," Sean said.

"Well, let's try it this way. Can you explain why witches have been set on various of the villagers? Specifically, and again, most of your enemies?" Ailís asked not at all sweetly.

"Coincidence?" Sean asked and began to perspire on a coolish fall day.

Ailís turned in the doorway, pointed to a group of passing witches and said, "You."

A witch dutifully approached.

"Do you know this man?" Ailís demanded pointing at Sean.

The witch peeked around the doorway and waved to Sean who closed his eyes and began to gnaw on his lip. "Yes, ma'am. That's Mr. Maher," the witch said.

"And has this man ever had any discussion with you and your friends about witches and druids and the like?" Ailís asked as Sean began to pray.

"Oh yes. He has pointed out a number of them to us, not that it did us much good, but we keep trying," the witch said as Sean decided there was no God for people like him.

"I see. I thank you for your assistance even though Mr. Maher doesn't," Ailís said.

"And what was it about this scheme that recommended itself to you?" Ailís asked Sean.

She stepped inside the station and closed the door behind her.

"Now, doctor darlin', Oi can explain. Why there is nothing to it a'tall," Sean began. "First of all, you mustn't believe foreigners.

Second, when you say Oi put one villager against another, why, you're just talking about a bit of fun. Nothing to that a'tall, Oi tell you."

"Don't bother, Sean. I will tell you this only because you are the nominal police presence in Cappel Vale, I admire your poor wife, and I would like to avoid bloodshed.

"Even the dimmest villager will figure out your shenanigans given enough time," Ailís said. "Well before that though, a large group of your fellow citizens will gather outside your door. Thereupon, they will hoist your guts on a pike," Ailís said and Sean winced.

"I will be unable to assist you. Pike related injuries are outside my area of expertise."

Before she left the police station, Ailís said and smiled her evilest smile, "By the way, Moira is looking for you."

\* \* \*

"What are we goin' to do?" the young woman whispered. Regardless of its rough walls and its few remaining worn pews, the monastery's chapel inspired hushed tones.

"Aileen, I tell ya, I don' know. Your da is huntin' for us and that's sure," the young man said.

"Da has a temper on him," Aileen said. "And it is worse when he is with drink taken. He'll kill us surely, Liam."

"Are you sorry you ran away with me?" Liam asked.

"You know I'm not, but, you were right. We should have asked me da first," Aileen said. "What'll we do if he finds us?"

"If? Don't ya mean when?" Liam said. "We're sittin' ducks here, but I couldn't think of another place to go."

A voice whispered out of the darkness. "Think of this as sanctuary."

Aileen and Liam went ashen before Liam called out more resolutely than he felt, "Who's there? Show yourself right now."

The voice materialized into a shadow at the back of the chapel, but no more was seen. "Just a friend. It looks like you two could use a friend just now."

"We don't need friends we can't see. Show yourself," Aileen said.

"No," the voice whispered.

"Why, not?" Liam demanded.

"Because you are in my chapel and because I like it better like this," the voice said.

"Well, we don't like it at all," Liam shouted.

"What you do and do not like is immaterial. Aileen's father is coming and will be here soon. If you want a friend, I can help. If you don't, you can go." The whisper bounced off the stone walls and found its way to the arched roof.

"If her da is coming, there is nothing to be done," Liam said.

"Don't be too sure. He is coming, but won't arrive for a bit. Why don't you tell me your story?" the voice asked.

"We've run away. We want to get married. Me da hates Liam and when he finds us, he'll kill us both," Aileen said.

"You don't need to tell 'im anything, Aileen. Let's just run for it," Liam said.

"Run now and you'll be running forever," the voice said.

"Oh? And what fine suggestion do you have?" Liam demanded.

"Aileen, what is your father's name? His given name," the voice murmured.

"Rory. What a daft thing to ask," Aileen said.

The thought rang out. "*He is here. Do nothing. Say nothing. Do you understand? No matter what, do not move, do not speak.*" Aileen and Liam felt the words rather than heard them and they looked at each other for confirmation before nodding their assent.

Minutes ticked by, announced by the steady drip of water from the roof's eves. Evening settled in and the chapel became deathly quiet before the door was kicked open.

A large man in a barn coat and field cap stood in the doorway silhouetted in the failing light outside. Cradled in his arms was a double barreled shotgun.

"You!" the man said. "You'll be dead and she'll be in a nunnery before this night is through." He took two long strides into the chapel.

"Welcome, Rory. Come in," the voice said, "but leave the shotgun at the door. This is a chapel after all."

"It's a building and nothing more. It hasn't been a chapel for fifty years, but it is the last place that bastard will ever see alive."

"The shotgun, Rory," the voice said.

"Show yourself. I've two barrels and as soon empty both as one," Rory said.

"You'll empty neither. If you would like to speak with your daughter, set down the shotgun now. Otherwise, depart now." The voice had changed sides of the chapel and Rory reacted by bringing the muzzle to bear.

"Stay out of me way. I've a job of work to do," Rory growled.

*"I can't do that."* Rory felt the words and froze.

The twin muzzles began to glow red hot. The big man dropped the weapon and it clattered to the floor of the chapel. His eyes became large and his nostrils flared as he scanned the chapel for the voice that tormented him.

Julian stepped from the shadows and walked casually forward. "Rory, do you love your daughter?" Julian whispered and canted his head to one side.

"Who are you and what business is it of yours?" the man demanded.

"Answer the important question, for you, the most important question. Do you love your daughter? Look at her and then answer my question," Julian said.

The big man looked to the altar rail and his face softened when he saw Aileen. "She is my world. Since her ma died, she is all I have."

"I know that, but do you love her?" Julian asked again. "Look at her, see her for the young woman she has become, the young woman you raised and nurtured."

"Of course I do. I just said so," Rory answered.

"Well, no you didn't. You said she was your world," Julian whispered. "She is all you have to remember your wife by," Julian said.

"It is time. You know it and I know it," Julian said. "It is the nature of children to leave, to make a home and family of their own. And it is time for you to carry on," Julian said. "It's what parents do and have always done."

The stiffening wind outside stirred the chapel not at all. Inside, several lonely souls sought the chapel's strength and that of a stranger. They sought sanctuary. Aileen and Liam dared to hope. Rory mourned the past and looked to a darkening road forward. Julian waited.

"She is all I have," Rory whispered.

"But she is not all you will have. She has been your past and your present. It is time to let her go. She will bring you grandchildren. She will bring you the future, your future," Julian said.

"Aileen, Liam, it is time to take your father home," Julian said. He patted Rory on the arm and the subtle charge of electricity calmed and warmed the big man.

* * *

"Sitting in church in the dead of night, Ailís?" Sr. Eugenia asked.

Ailís jumped. "Oh sister, I didn't see you. You startled me. How long have you been there?"

"Long enough to see you wipe away your tears," the nun said with a kind smile that broke laugh lines at her eyes. "Tell me what I can do."

"I'm afraid there is nothing to be done," Ailís whispered.

"Oh my, I am afraid that simply won't do. Nothing to be done? There is always something to be done about nearly everything." Sr. Eugenia was a stately, cultured, rail thin nun who ran the village school with an iron fist sans the velvet glove. She didn't want anything to lessen the blow.

The nun gathered her skirt and sat in the pew next to Ailís.

"This is the first place Julian and I had a real conversation. I must have talked for an hour. He couldn't have slid in a word on edge if he wanted to. He didn't want to, of course. He felt, rightly it turns out, I needed to talk. He was so kind, so caring, so tender with me. I can't help but cry when I think of that night," Ailís said.

"He is also pig headed and insanely secretive. That night, I asked him questions about himself. He talked, but managed to say almost nothing," Ailís said.

"I would wager you know him a wee bit better now, my dear," the nun said.

Ailís smiled and her face flushed, but she said nothing.

"It is common knowledge Julian was injured while in Rome. Is he healing quickly? I do hope so," Sr. Eugenia said.

Ailís knew the nun would ask the one question the doctor could not answer.

"My dear?" the older woman said.

Ailís slumped in the pew. She looked at the tabernacle behind the altar, closed her eyes and said, "I don't know if he is healing. I don't know when he'll be back or even if."

"Well, I'm sure things are progressing as they should for you both. It would be good to have Julian home soon though. He is a dear man in many ways, although prone to mischief," the nun said and her smiled warmed Ailís.

✳ ✳ ✳

# Chapter Seventeen

The first charge of electricity Julian sent out scythed a dead tree in half. The next halved it again. And in half again. And again.

"Hello there, Finbar," Julian said moments before the rumpled old man appeared.

"I can't tell you how happy I am you have found something useful to do with your talents. It would be such a loss if you wasted them. Tell me, lad, have you taken up chopping wood for a living or are you just punishing that poor tree for some transgression?" Finbar asked and scowled.

"Feeling a bit cranky today, are we?" Julian said.

"Indeed I am. I am not a patient man and this waiting for Manning is wearing on me," Finbar said in a better frame of mind.

Julian reached out with his mind and began to stack the cleanly cut logs. "I've compiled everything you've said and everything I've learned. It isn't so much a matter of patience. It is all about waiting 'til the time is right. I can rush it and chance I'll get the timing wrong or I can wait for the proper time to arrive. I suppose it is a matter of making it happen or letting it happen as and when it should, no?" Julian said.

"Well, aren't we feeling all philosophical this fine day," Finbar said and smirked. "It is grossly unfair that you are horribly rational while I am jumping out of my skin with the anxiety."

"Don't get me wrong, Finbar. There was another bombing today. Another phone call to the police with my name prominently mentioned. It is hard to wait, my friend. Very hard and very painful, but wait we shall, eh?"

"I hate it when you're reasonable," Finbar said.

"All part of my charm," Julian responded and ground his teeth in the frustration of waiting.

* * *

"Out for an amble?" Moira asked Ailís when the two met on the main thoroughfare of Cappel Vale.

"Just wanted to get out and stretch my legs," Ailís answered.

"And how is it for you?" Moira asked.

"Everything is just fine, thank you for asking." Ailís' reply was terse.

"What, no tale of woe?" Moira asked.

"If you will remember, you said you would take a switch to me if I talked to you about, well, certain things," Ailís said and made a face at the older woman.

"Besides, I really don't think of it much anymore so your advice proved useful this time. A rarity to be sure," Ailís said.

"What a liar you are and not even a very good one. Why, any child could out lie you," Moira said and cackled.

"A fat lot you know about anything, Moira Hagan," Ailís said. "Every word is true.

"No phone calls, no letters, not a peep do I hear from that dreadful man. I am done with him I tell you," Ailís said with heat in her voice and color rising on her cheeks.

"Never give him a moment's thought, is it? It is all that is on that tiny brain of yours," Moira said and a smile cut across her face.

"That is a filthy lie!" Ailís shouted.

"Well then, what has you so distracted these days?" Moira asked pleasantly.

"I'm not a bit distracted," Ailís answered. "I'm at the top of my game since I put this foolishness behind me."

"Well, tell me why you prescribed David O'Connor something to take care of his menstrual cramps instead of his hemorrhoids? How about little Tommy Quinn? He broke his left arm and you put a cast on the right. Novel treatments I must say. Top of your game is it? Ha!" Moira said with a grin.

"If you get any more on top of your game, we'll have to have a doctor come in to fix all your doctoring. The good news is, at least you've stopped your constant bleating about Julian Blessing," Moira said and left a seething Dr. Ailís Dwyer in the street.

\* \* \*

"Welcome to my home, Inspector. Please, come in and tell me how I can be of assistance to An Garda Síochána," Bridget Bragonier said.

Flannigan followed her through to the front room. The cut crystal lamps sparkled, reflecting light off dark mahogany end tables. The rest of the room was softly bathed in shades of white.

"May I offer you tea?" Bridget asked and showered Flannigan with a dazzling smile.

"No ma'am, nothing for me," Flannigan said.

"Well then, tell me the nature of your visit and I will see what I can do to be of help," Bridget said and looked into the inspector.

Flannigan backed away from his hostess when he noticed her pearl gray eyes and felt the intensity of her stare. He had seen this before. Julian Blessing's eyes were a different gray, but his look was no less penetrating. Bridget's smile widened when she was done inspecting the inspector.

"Mrs. Bragonier, as I said on the telephone, I am seeking information on two men. Julian Blessing and a…" Flannigan consulted his notes, "Mr. Manning."

"Where would you like to start, Inspector?" Bridget asked.

"It would probably be best to start with Manning since I know nothing about him," Flannigan said.

"The man you have identified as Manning is the former Terrance Cardinal Patrick Manning. He was in charge of the Vatican Bank and managed to swindle the Church for one billion Euros. In the process he left a path of unrestrained human destruction. I believe INTERPOL would like to have a chat with him. I can assure you, that conversation will never take place.

"He is in Ireland when last I heard. I believe he is with a man named John Clarke. Inspector, both of these men are without conscience. They will murder anyone who stands in their way. Should you meet either of them, run the other way and pray they don't see you. You will not survive the encounter otherwise," Bridget said. "He has murdered before. He will continue to do so until he is stopped."

"Get in the way of what, Mrs. Bragioner? What are they after in Ireland?" Flannigan asked.

"I'm afraid I really could not say." Bridget smiled.

"I can tell you Julian harbors an intense hatred for Mr. Manning. As far as Julian is concerned, there are scores that need to be settled and an evil that needs to be stopped. Still, have a care Inspector and do not interfere with Julian as he handles this."

"Thank you for your advice, ma'am, but I'm afraid I cannot allow Mr. Blessing to interfere with the apprehension of criminals in the Republic. Still, I will pass along your warning to my superintendent.

"As to the other, I am working with Mr. Blessing. I understand you know him well," the inspector said.

"Indeed, it is my great pleasure to know him," Bridget said.

"I was wondering what you could tell me about him. It would help me to be better able to either assist him or for him to be of assistance to me. Anything you can tell me would be a help," Inspector Flannigan said and smiled hopefully.

The room they were sitting in told him volumes about its owner. Tasteful, arranged artfully and perfectly accessorized. The artwork on the walls and on plinths near the windows were expensive without being gaudy or pretentious. The dull daylight filtered into the room. Flannigan couldn't figure out if the room enhanced the meager daylight or his hostess did.

Formidable, elegant, bordering on stately with a keen mind, a perfect hostess' smile and eyes that pinned him like a bug to a corkboard – that is how he would later describe Mrs. Bridget Bragonier.

"There is some reason you are asking me and not him?"

"Since you know him, you know he is, I would have to say, reticent to talk about himself. I want to be able to assist him to the best of my ability. To do that, I feel I need to know him better," Flannigan said and could feel sweat running down his spine.

Bridget looked at and into Inspector Flannigan for a full minute. What she saw was a well-educated, well-mannered young man. His stated reason for being in her best room was true.

"Inspector, I believe you. That is, you have not lied to me, but you've not told me everything, have you?" Bridget asked.

"Mrs. Bragonier?"

"You will be required to report back to your superiors everything that is said and done here. Is that not true? Perhaps I can get you a whiskey?"

"Yes ma'am. I mean, no ma'am. That is…yes, I will be required to report the gist of our conversation to my superintendent. A word-for-word accounting will not be rendered though. It is very kind of you, but no whiskey for me," Flannigan said having never wanted a drink more.

Bridget walked to the sideboard where she poured a stiff Jameson 18 Vintage Reserve Irish whiskey. She handed it to Flannigan as she swept back to her chair.

"Very well, I will tell you what I know and you can pick and choose what will help you and what will not and what you will report to your superiors. Does that not seem fair?" Bridget asked.

"Yes ma'am, very fair," Flannigan said.

"As you say, Julian is a rather private person. I doubt anyone ever knows exactly what he is thinking and what he is doing need not be what he is really doing. Is this getting confusing yet?" Bridget asked, tilted her head and smiled.

"Yes, ma'am, it is all very confusing. You are saying there is no way to know him?"

"Exactly. No need to worry though. No one knows him because he is a man of many, many facets. He presents a different aspect of himself to different people. In this way, he is not unlike you."

"Like me, Mrs. Bragioner?"

"In some ways, yes. Think of it this way. You are uniquely able to mix well in any company. You can speak to the criminal element, the citizenry, your peers and your superiors each in their own language. You present a different façade depending on the circumstances. There is nothing deceptive about this. You blend in well. Believe me, you will go far in your chosen profession because of this talent," Bridget said and continued her story.

"I met Julian in New York. I knew he was special from our first meeting. I have grown to know how special over time.

"He was a man in transition at the time of our meeting. He was in the process of leaving his chosen field and looking for something else. My husband and I encouraged him to visit Ireland. He agreed and ended up making his home in Cappel Vale. Doubtless, the details of his time there are in a police report somewhere," Bridget said.

The inspector looked at the pattern in the Persian rug and concentration cut deep lines into his forehead. "Those are the facts, ma'am, but they don't address my needs. How is he special?" Flannigan asked.

"First of all, he has a truly original mind. He looks at the world differently than the rest of us. He is inventive, intuitive and, most of all, unpredictable.

"As I said, like you, Julian is able to mix in all sorts of company. In his village, he is universally loved and respected. Laborers, medical professionals, farm wives and the landed gentry seek out his opinion and his help on things.

"Under normal circumstances, I would advise you to interview his friends and neighbors. That, however, would be very bad advice indeed. You see, Julian engenders extreme loyalty. Any of the villagers would lay down their life for him. I assure you, you would receive a severe beating or worse should you attempt to pry into his affairs. If you do, please bring the riot squad. You will need them if you hope to escape alive." Bridget smiled a glittering smile.

"You are special like Mr. Blessing, aren't you?" Flannigan said flatly and with a boldness he did not feel.

"You and I may be using the word 'special' differently. In what way do you mean Julian and I are special?" Bridget said.

Having dug a hole, he continued to dig. "I have noted Mr. Blessing knows thing he couldn't possibly know, for example. That is a talent you share, but I suspect there are other talents," Flannigan said and held his breath.

"What next, Inspector Flannigan? The bright light and the rubber truncheon? I must say, if I am going to be interrogated, doing so in my own living room is preferable to your dungeons at Phoenix Park," Bridget said naming An Garda Síochána's headquarters. She smiled her best hostess smile and Flannigan nearly melted.

"Madam, if I have left the impression this an interrogation, I am sincerely sorry. This is an interview only so that…"

"Yes, so that you will be better able to assist Mr. Blessing. You've said that several times. Another whiskey?"

"No, thank you," Flannigan said and could feel his courage leaving him.

"I will say only this, Inspector. I am, as you can see, an old woman. Over my many years I have known many, many people from all walks of life. Some, it has been a privilege to know. Knowing some has been distasteful. Most people however fall in the middle of that spectrum," Bridget began.

"With time and patience and practice, I have developed a skill. I am able to know, to a high probability, what people will and will not do.

"Julian however, approaches it differently. He has a native ability to see into people, to read them as it were. It is instinctive for him. So, while I must practice, Julian does it effortlessly. Does that answer your question, young man?" Bridget said.

Flannigan took a deep breath, set his Waterford crystal glass on a coaster and rolled the dice. "Mrs. Bragonier." The inspector felt as though his hostess' gray eyes were boring a hole into his head. She said nothing.

"I'm sorry, but I feel as though I am asking the wrong questions. What should I be asking?" Flannigan said.

"You are honest and that counts for quite a bit with me. When you arrived, you said you wanted to be of assistance to Julian and so needed to understand him. Those are exclusive statements. You should have stated the first as a question and forgotten about the second part," Bridget said with kindness.

"How can Mr. Blessing and I be of assistance to each other?" Flannigan asked.

"In order to assist him, you need not understand him. However, your association can be mutually beneficial if you are willing to do one thing. It is simplicity itself really," Bridget said.

"You must trust him in all things. If he says a thing is true, trust that it is. If he suspects something is going to unfold a certain way, know that it will. He will never command, but if he asks you to do something, do it immediately. Do not hesitate and do not question him. He will explain when the time is right. You may believe me; you will be rewarded for your trust.

"Never underestimate him and never think to cross him, Inspector," Bridget said and activated the laugh lines at the corners of her eyes with her smile. "You may trust too that Julian is full of surprises and capable of all sorts of mischief," Bridget said.

"May I ask a personal question, Mrs. Bragonier? A deeply personal question. Please feel free to refuse to answer. Anything you say is strictly off the record," Flannigan said.

"Ask your question. I may answer. I may not."

"Do you have the sight?"

Bridget considered a long time before saying, "Yes."

"Does Mr. Blessing?" Flannigan asked.

"No," Bridget answered.

"I don't know anything about your gift other than folk tales. Can you not see the next target for the bomber or where Mr. Manning can be found?" Flannigan asked.

"Those are very good questions, young man. Believe me, if I could see into this murky business, I would give you whatever information I had gleaned. There is a sort of mist shrouding the present and the future with regard to these incidents. This is unusual, but has happened before. Someone is keeping me from seeing anything related to this business and that someone is Mr. Manning."

"Do you feel this Manning is behind the bombings?" Flannigan asked.

"I do," Bridget said.

"Then Manning is like you and Mr. Blessing? I mean he is special like you two."

"You may be sure, Mr. Manning is like us only in that he wields certain powers. You may also be sure we are polar opposites in all other ways," Bridget said.

"Thank you, Mrs. Bragonier. You have been generous with your time and I sincerely appreciate it."

Bridget inclined her head and nodded once slowly.

Flannigan stood and said, "Please don't disturb yourself, I can see myself out."

He had nearly reached the front door when Bridget's thoughts entered his head and he froze. *"Inspector Flannigan, if you make the right choices, you will have a brilliant career. One of those choices should be to think of Julian as a friend rather than a resource. Good day to you and do feel free to call on me at any time."*

Flannigan was on the other side of the door when he felt the afterthought. *"By the way, when you ask that girl of yours, she will say yes. She is a brilliant choice. Besides, how could she refuse your charm?"*

✳ ✳ ✳

# Chapter Eighteen

The young man was seated in a well-appointed library in a stately Edwardian home on St. Stephen's Green. Behind an enormous carved oak desk sat Terrance Manning. John Clarke draped himself in a nearby club chair and thumbed through a magazine.

"Well, haven't you been a busy fellow," Manning said. "Entirely too busy for my tastes. Please tell me why I shouldn't kill you."

Fear animated every atom of the young man. He thought he would be dealing with someone far more sympathetic to his cause.

"Mr. Manning," the young man began.

"Ah, you know my name. How nice. I don't need to know yours as you probably won't be with us that much longer."

"Sir," the young man began again. "Our government is a cesspool of corruption, deceit and self-interest. There is no one on the horizon who will address what ails the nation," the young man began.

"So," Manning interjected, "the government of the republic is like any other government and you're not getting your share of the fruits of its labor?" Manning looked at and into the young man and knew he was right.

This was not a man of high moral principles. Social justice was not his motivation. Like most people, Manning thought, this man was motivated by avarice.

"In one hundred and fifty words, you had better tell me what you want and why you believe I can grant your wish. Please, remember you are fighting for your life. I hope that doesn't make you nervous."

The young man swallowed hard and organized his thoughts. Clarke looked up from his magazine with something approximating interest.

"Gentlemen, I believe I can be of assistance to you. I have already captured the imagination of the population and the attention of the government. If I am correct, you are preparing to destabilize the country and the economy. You are going to first attack and then replace Ireland's social and political fabric.

"If allowed to continue, I believe I am ideally suited to distract the government while you go about your business unseen by the authorities.

"Once you have attained your goals, I would expect to be rewarded for the part I've played. Once I've completed my task and have been compensated, well, we are done," the young man said as perspiration stood out on his forehead. His palms were moist and his legs shook beneath his trousers. "You can kill me with impunity, but I believe I am worth more to you alive than dead."

"John, what think you of our young friend's proposal?" Manning asked.

"Kill him," Clarke answered matter-of-factly.

"You really are too quick to kill things. We can kill him at a time and place of our choosing should things transpire in a way that doesn't fit our purposes.

"Young man, you can continue to live and to blow things up. In fact, it would be helpful to tie the authorities up in knots while we pursue our plans. I admire your initiative in trying to link Julian Blessing to the bombings. Wish I'd thought of that myself," Manning said.

"Should you complete your task admirably, indeed you will be duly rewarded," Manning said and smiled.

"As to the other – lad, we are done when you are dead. Let's not forget that." Manning's smile broadened and Clarke looked genuinely pleased.

\* \* \*

"What do you mean, you didn't learn much!" Superintendent Murphy shouted.

"Sir, Mrs. Bragonier is a remarkably complex woman. She has a talent for saying almost nothing and using a lot of words to say it," Inspector Flannigan said. "That is not to say I didn't learn anything. I just don't know the value of what I did learn."

"Does Mrs. Bragonier have the second sight? Yes, or no, if you please," Murphy asked.

"Yes," Flannigan answered.

"Does Blessing?"

"No."

"Can he help us with this case?"

"Oh yes," the inspector said. "He is the key to it all."

* * *

"Blessing is proving especially difficult," Manning said to his protégé, John Clarke.

"Difficult in what way this time?" Clarke asked.

"I expected he would rise to the bait and come looking for us. That is proving not to be the case. Doubtless, his restraint is the result of Mr. Clancy's influence," Manning said.

"Well then, problem solved. I will go visit with Blessing and his dwarf and I will draw this difficult episode to a close," Clarke said.

"You will not. At this point, we will go to him. Early on it mattered. I wanted him to come to us, to join us, but that time has passed. Now there is nothing for it but to eliminate him. You, however, are not to engage him. His time is coming, but we have others items on our agenda that take precedence," Manning said.

* * *

"No, no, no," Finbar said. "How many times do we have to go over this? You have all the finesse of a meat cleaver.

"Rather than try to swamp your opponent with sheer brute force, become tightly focused on small weak spots. Julian, lad, you've come far, but now it is time to leave behind the muscular nature of your attacks. Concentrate on the fine points of each assault.

"Now get back there and we'll try again," Finbar said and let out a noisy breath.

The old man moderated his tone and continued, saying, "Julian, I don't know how you can intensify your training. There is little left I can teach you."

"Well, if you're tired, I understand," Julian said and suppressed a smile.

"Tired is it??!! I may be old, but I can still do you a treat or two. Now get over there and prepare to be punished for your cheekiness," Finbar said.

"Don't worry, old man. I know how frail you are," Julian said. "Rather than go way over there, I'll just stay here. Twenty feet should be enough, don't you think? I'll take it easy on you."

"The only thing you're going to take is the back of me hand, ya eejit," Finbar shouted. "Twenty feet? Make it ten, boyo and hope you are fast enough."

"Ten it is. Brave talk for someone in his dotage, no?" Julian asked.

"No more of your sass. Get over here and shut your gob. We'll see exactly what you have left to learn. Today's lesson is humility!" Finbar said.

The first bout lasted for five exchanges. Finbar laughed and Julian snorted. The second and all subsequent assaults lasted two exchanges. Julian smiled and Finbar swore after each one.

The old man was on his knees wheezing with the effort. "Ready to give up?" he asked.

"What was it you were saying about humility?" Julian asked.

"Who, me? I don't remember saying anything of the sort," Finbar said as he picked himself up.

"Julian, me boy, I want to warn you about something. I've seen you practicing stepping in and out of time along with some other clever tricks. They will be worthless against Manning and Clarke," Finbar said.

"They, and you, are too clever for any of that. This will be a battle to be sure, but the winner will be the best strategist. Just remember, finesse and strategy and drawing strength from outside yourself will carry the day. Perfect the basics and you'll be fine," Finbar said.

Julian turned to retrieve their coats from a nearby stump. Finbar fired a barrage that traveled out five feet and bounced back.

"You cagey bastard. That hurt!" Finbar said.

Julian laughed for the first time in months.

"The student becomes the master. That's as it always has been, how it should be," Finbar whispered to himself. "I won't mention it to him though. He already knows."

* * *

"Reginald, please do not touch that." Something in his wife's voice caused Professor Reginald Bragonier to pull up short of the mail that had dropped through the slot in the door of their home.

Bridget stared at the small pile of envelopes and circulars. The corner of a thick manila envelope stuck out from the rest of the mail. Bridget said, "Please, back away from there and use the phone on the sideboard in your study to call emergency services.

"I will go to the street and await their arrival. Once you have made your call, go to garden and wait for me. I will join you as soon as I can.

"You may tell them we have received a letter bomb," Bridget said.

# Chapter Nineteen

Julian again stood on the cliff's edge. He looked out to sea and tried to lift the heavy curtain Manning had wrapped around his thoughts. Julian examined the fabric and the folds looking for a way in, some small opening that would allow him to see clearly.

"Finbar, the Book said to shine the light of reason into the darkness of unreason. I am to illuminate the unreality and the darkness will vanish. The Jesuit Book instructed to not be confused by what isn't there."

"But how?" Julian whispered. "How do I know what isn't there?"

"It's right in front of you," Finbar said. "You keep looking out to sea trying to peer into the future, but you are on a fool's errand. You will never pierce the future without knowing where you have been. Search the past. Draw together the threads of where you have been, where Manning has been.

"He is a powerful man, to be sure, but he can't be everywhere at once. He can cover the future and shroud the present, but he can't suppress the past," Finbar said.

"Focus your mind. The talents you've been given have been given to you for a reason. Use them, lad," the old man said and he watched as Julian turned his gaze back out over the Irish Sea.

Finbar was right, it was there. Just on the fringes of a distracting present and a clouded future.

With a sudden start Julian stood straighter. He could feel it. A tiny crack appeared in Manning's armor.

Julian concentrated. He forced himself to turn the full weight of his awareness onto a single point. His eyes were closed tightly and his hands curled into tense fists. The muscles of his arms, shoulders and neck corded with the strain.

There it was. Laid out before him was the how and why and, most of all, the who of it all.

Julian slumped, then fell to his knees, exhausted from the concentration.

He had it. He had the answers he sought. He knew.

He smiled and shook his head.

"Speak to me lad," Finbar said around his pipe and with a smile on his wizened face. "The Irish, we have a talent for turning good news into bad, so do your worst. Let's see if I can talk you out of your new found euphoria, eh?" Finbar said.

"All this time. I was looking in the wrong place all this time," Julian began.

"Manning shut down anyone with second sight by clouding the future. Bridget was effectively blinded. He cast a thick fog over the present. You, me, none of us could see clearly. He did the same thing in Rome. The man is nothing if not powerful enough to direct the darkness," Julian said.

"I'm sure you thought I was nuts standing out here. I'm sure everyone thought I was nuts. Admit it, you thought so, Finbar."

"No, I just thought you were looking for something. As to how insane others might find you, well now isn't that a foregone conclusion?" Finbar said.

"All I needed to do was look for something else and it would have been right in front of me. How could I be so stupid!" Julian shouted at the sea.

"How stupid is it? Well, I suppose you were born that way," Finbar said. "Listen sharp, lad. This has not been wasted time. You have employed your time wisely by honing your skills, by getting ready. Tell me though, what is it you found?"

"Everything. Manning forgot about the past. He threw a shade over it. Nearly covered it, but not quite.

"Looking into the past is one of the things I can do. I can't see what Manning is doing, but I can see what he has done. I can't tell what the bomber will do, but I can see him as he spread his path of destruction.

"The past, Finbar. It is all right there in the past. All the predictors of what will take place in the future. They are right there. The echoes, for me, they are not from the future or the present. They are from the past," Julian said in triumph.

"I need only remove one piece from the puzzle Manning is assembling. It won't bring down the whole thing, but it will be enough," Julian said.

"I have counseled you to be careful when you wanted to be reckless. I have advised you to be patient when that is the last thing you wanted. I was afraid for you. Afraid you weren't sufficiently fortified for the fight ahead. Lad, I have only one more thing to say," Finbar said and put away his pipe.

"You are ready."

\* \* \*

In a strained voice Bridget said, "Julian, it would seem Mr. Manning is trying to lure you out by escalating the violence and by making this extremely personal. I would not have called otherwise."

"You have received a bomb in the mail," Julian said into the telephone. "I should have known, should have been able to warn you. I'm sorry," Julian said.

"You were no more capable of seeing into this business than was I," Bridget said.

"But that's not true, Bridget. Had I paid attention, had I studied, had I focused, I would have known. I know now and we can expect no other surprises from Manning," Julian said.

"Julian, what has changed?" Bridget asked and concern cut deep ridges in her voice.

"Everything," Julian answered and hung up the phone.

\* \* \*

"Taoiseach, I would like to see you as soon as possible," Julian said. He was sitting at Dr. Mahoney's desk, the telephone in his left hand and fatigue touching his eyes.

"You have something for me then?" Connelly asked. "I will send a car and driver to pick you up. He will be there soon." The telephone call ended abruptly.

\* \* \*

Inspector Flannigan drove in silence, the rumble of the tires on the road the only sound.

"How do you keep getting so lucky, Inspector? I mean, to be assigned to drive me into Dublin in this case," Julian said and nearly smiled.

"I've been working with you right along, sir," the inspector said. "They thought you would be more comfortable with someone you knew.

"I see. So everyone else refused again and you were the one who got stuck with me," Julian said.

"Well, sir," Flannigan looked sheepish. "Yes. At least in the beginning. Now, I want to do it. I want to know."

"Know?"

"Yes, sir. You are different, special. You have talents and I need to understand them," the inspector said. "It is important to my career, but more importantly, it is important to me."

"One of these days, we'll sit down and have a long conversation. However, for now, you have nothing to fear. Your days of being the goat are behind you," Julian said.

Inspector Flannigan navigated the dense Dublin traffic and parked the car. Julian got out, but the inspector stayed behind the wheel.

"Coming?" Julian asked.

"Sir, my orders were to pick you up and deliver you here. Afterwards, I am to take you back or wherever you want to go," Flannigan answered.

Julian sighed. "Inspector, what is your first name?"

"Kevin, sir. Kevin Flannigan."

"Good, Kevin. I am not sir or mister. I am Julian. You said you wanted to understand. This is how it's done. You can either disregard your orders and accept my invitation or I will ask the Taoiseach to send for you. Your choice, but either way you are about to become famous."

Flannigan locked the car and followed Julian down the palatial hallways of the epicenter of the Republic's power and powerful. He felt his career was over before it began and thought how disappointed his family would be.

Julian checked in with Connelly's secretary, Thomas Ahern. The man seemed nervous, but advised Julian the Taoiseach was waiting for him.

When he entered, Connelly was seated behind his desk and Edward Brennen, his assistant, was in a guest chair. Both men stood as Julian and the inspector entered.

"*Kevin, as they say, stay alert and stay alive. Things may get dicey at any moment,*" Julian thought and Flannigan's eyes went large.

Switching back to the spoken word, Julian said, "Taoiseach, thank you for seeing me. I am sorry I couldn't give you proper notice, but felt you would want an update as soon as possible."

"My door is always open to you, Mr. Blessing," Connelly lied easily. "Please, introduce me to your associate."

"Sir, this is Inspector Kevin Flannigan. I am assisting him with the investigation," Julian said.

"I can assume you have news?" Connelly said.

"I do sir. Your bomber is not acting alone. He is in league with a man named Manning."

"Wait, I know of Manning. He was a cardinal in Rome. He was from right here in Dublin. Something to do with the Vatican bank. But he died in a fire at the airport. You are saying he didn't?" Connelly asked.

"I can assure you he did not. I can assure you he is not controlling, but is allowing these bombings. I can assure you also the bomber working with Manning is Edward Brennen."

Brennen bolted for the door, but Flannigan tackled him before he made it half way.

"Inspector, please place Mr. Brennen under arrest, but call your dispatcher and have your prisoner transported under heavy guard."

Flannigan looked quizzical but nodded once as the handcuffs ratcheted closed on Brennen's wrists. The inspector searched the man before wrestling him into a chair.

Connelly sat stunned and was only shaken out of his daze when several members of the emergency response unit arrived and took possession of the prisoner.

"But Edward was with me for years. His loyalty was always unquestioned."

Julian noticed Connelly was already referring to Brennen in the past tense. In politics, when life gives you a lemon, distance yourself as soon as and as far as possible and swear you always hated lemons.

"So many deaths - what was the point?" Connelly asked.

"His object was serving two masters," Julian said. "On the one hand, the best way to advancement is to be the last person standing. The second was to assist Manning in undermining the government. In both cases, the best way to do that was to sow terror in the minds of the general population.

"Brennen focused on attention-getting targets, but you can bet it would have led to a large gathering of citizens. A football match, I would guess, where hundreds would have died," Julian said.

"When their leaders can't protect the people, the people will find leaders who can. You can guess the rest," Julian said.

"How did you know?" Connelly asked. "I'm sorry I asked that. So, Edward was leaking information to the news outlets too?"

"In fact, Brennen was not doing that," Julian said.

"You have discovered who is?"

"Yes, Taoiseach."

"And?"

"Everyone is leaking including you," Julian said.

"But that isn't…" Connelly began to lie.

"Isn't it. Taoiseach?" Julian cut in. "Every kickback or questionable practice that can be attributed to your leadership was followed the next day by some tidbit of embarrassing personal information about someone other than you. Beyond that, I know because I know and what I know is your entire cabinet leaks like an old church roof," Julian said.

\* \* \*

"You, Grayhawk, come here," Moira commanded.

"Who, me?" Lavonia asked as she trudged up the main street in Cappel Vale.

"You're the only Grayhawk I see, ya nit," Moira said.

Lavonia, with hands shaking and sweaty palms, presented herself.

"You have work to do," Moira began. "You're to take over the Solis Luna coven and fold 'em into your own."

"Yeahbut, I can't do that," Lavonia said. "Lady Vanessa…"

"Oh, so many things are wrong with you. First of all, that Vanessa Warden person has hoofed it, so her coven is currently without a chief-witch-in-charge. Second, I wasn't making a request. Now get to it, girl," Moira said.

"Yeahbut I can't. I'm not qualified to…"

Moira sighed. *"I'm feeling in a benevolent mood today,"* she thought and with crystal clarity the words rang in Lavonia's head and she began to shake. Moira continued, *"Because of this, I will explain things in simple terms.*

*"You may have noticed, I'm not a witch. Still, I've known plenty who are. They are a proud lot who all have some things in common. It is the thing you are about to develop yourself and do so quickly,"* Moira thought.

*"They have all found their place in the universe and claimed it for their own. I've also noted, witches have a deep seated sense of responsibility*

*for the welfare of others and a reverence for all life. Are you a witch or no? Are you play acting or are you someone to be taken seriously? Life is a series of choices. Time for you to make yours,"* Moira concluded.

"I'm afraid," Lavonia stammered.

*"Good. You should be. Being a witch does not come cheaply,"* Moira responded and waited as the younger woman worked out her decision.

Lavonia Grayhawk nodded once. That one gesture wedded her to the practice of witchcraft with all of its rewards and all of its responsibilities. "I'll just go out and collect the Solis Luna coven," she said with resolve.

Moira smiled and winked. "You do that. I have a not-so-white witch to hunt."

\* \* \*

"Sir, ah, Julian, that was the Taoiseach. How do you get away with talking to him like that?" Flannigan asked. He and Julian were walking down the long thickly carpeted hallway leading to the front entrance.

"Kevin, people are afraid of the unknown. I am the ultimate unknown quantity for people like Connelly," Julian answered. "He doesn't have a convenient box he can put me in, so I am set aside in a container marked dangerous. There are a few others in that box, I imagine. He hasn't figured out your part in this, so we're in the box together."

"How did you know it was Brennen? When can we get at this Manning character?" the inspector asked.

"I trusted my instincts and, as you saw, he revealed himself by running rather than denying," Julian said.

"What if you had been wrong?" Flannigan said.

"Then I would have looked like an eejit." Julian stressed the word and smiled.

"And Manning?" the inspector asked.

"There is no getting at him. Let's just hope you never meet him. Very few people survive the encounter."

"Sorry I have so many questions, but why did you want someone else to take Brennen to the lockup?" the inspector asked.

The smile dropped away and Julian's mouth turned hard. "Brennen will never make it to jail. He will die in route and no one will ever know why. I didn't want that to happen on your watch. You made the arrest. That's what will be remembered."

"But," Kevin asked, "how and why will he die? It's healthy enough he looked to me and he had some fight left in him."

"Manning," was Julian's answer.

* * *

The headache developed at the back of Bridget's head. It was always the way of things when visions of the future came to her.

She sat in her dining room across from her husband. "What can I do, my dear?" an alarmed Professor Bragioner asked. He need not have asked the source of the problem. He had seen it too often.

"There is nothing for it. When I get glimpses of the future, this never happens. It is only when I can see it clearly in its entirety the headaches come. Sadly, my darling, there is nothing you can do," Bridget said and smiled slightly.

With narrowed eyes, the professor asked and caution guided his words, "And what does the future hold?"

"Devastation and betrayal at the monastery, my dear, and death," Bridget answered and closed her eyes tightly against the pain.

\* \* \*

"Well, our Julian Blessing has been a busy boy," John Clarke said.

"Yes, I know. He captured our man in the office of the Taoiseach," Manning said.

"Do you want me to do something about the problem?" Clarke asked relishing the prospect.

"Hate to disappoint. I do know how you look forward to killing things, but Brennen has been disposed of. He was an asset, but always an unreliable one," Manning said.

Clarke asked, "And Blessing?"

Terrance Manning looked into the gloom of another overcast Dublin afternoon and sighed. "He will have to die, now, won't he," Manning said. "Call for the car if you would. We are going to deal with a problem that should have been seen to at the start."

\* \* \*

Flannigan could feel the tension radiate from Julian. No words were exchanged, but the inspector could feel the air charged with an electricity that made the hair on his arms stand up.

"Kevin, do you like being a policeman?" Julian asked.

"I do, yes. Oh, there are things I don't like about it, but that's the same with any job isn't it? Do you like doing what, ah, you do?" the inspector asked.

"You mean, 'whatever' it is you do? No need to answer. There are times I don't like what I have to do. It is necessary, but still…" Julian said, "tonight will be one of those nights, Kevin."

\* \* \*

Julian and Inspector Flannigan stood next to the burnt out shell of Finbar's cottage. The charred pages of books floated on currents of ash. The chimney remained standing, its blackened stones silhouetted against the dim late afternoon sun. The stone walls stood, brittle and broken by the intense heat. Hot spots still flared as they found the few remaining sources of fuel. The winds fanned them giving new life to the sparks.

The thatched roof had collapsed powering the spread of the fire and turning the interior into an inferno, baking or incinerating outright everything inside the small structure.

He could feel it at his core. Julian knew his tutor and friend had been present when the building burst into flames. He could feel something else. A distinct signature lingered in the air, one he would not forget or forgive.

"Kevin, you'll need to call this in and start the preliminary investigation. Stay here. I have something to take care of," Julian said and began to walk away.

"My chief superintendent would have my head! My instructions are to stay with you until Manning can be brought in," Kevin Flannigan said as he trotted to catch up.

Julian stopped and faced the inspector. The thought rang clearly in the young man's head. *"You don't seem to understand. Manning isn't just a criminal. He isn't going to be brought anywhere. The laws you enforce don't affect him in the least. You have no means or methods, no policies or procedures for dealing with someone like him. He is beyond your reach, out of your jurisdiction,"* Julian thought. *"But not mine.*

"Kevin, I suggest you stay here and do your job. If you have any interest in staying alive, do not interfere. I will be back or I won't," Julian said and smiled a slight smile.

The lights burned brightly in the doctor's office and a limousine was parked discreetly nearby, its driver behind the wheel.

The time had come. Julian set a resolute pace as he walked toward the monastery's chapel.

* * *

# Chapter Twenty

The chapel preserved its vow of silence. Its walls separated the calm, still interior from the harsh weather outside. It was a sanctuary for the weary and the weak, believers and nonbelievers alike. It was an island in the maelstrom of life. The only sounds were footsteps that approached without hurry.

"I felt that since you would not come to me, the only polite thing would be for me to come to you," Manning said. Clarke roughly pushed Dr. Mahoney ahead of him into the chapel.

Julian stood relaxed and with a slight smile. He whispered, "I can always count on you to do the polite thing. Murder is bad-mannered though, don't you think?"

"True. Regrettable at times perhaps, but necessary. How else could I get your attention?" Manning said as he stopped in the center of the nave. Clarke threw Mahoney to the stone floor, moved away and stood against the far wall.

"I don't know. A phone call? A letter perhaps?" Julian said. "Oh, I forgot, you are a man who needs the theatricality of the thing regardless of who it kills.

"I see you brought the doctor," Julian said. "He is how you knew my comings and goings and were able to follow my activities, of course," Julian said. "His signature gave him away early on. Strong emotions do that. His signature changed again after Clarke's first kill in the village. You remember, the farmer? Fear is a powerful emotion and it leaves an indelible mark."

"I swear to you Julian, I had no choice," the doctor said with tears streaming down his face as he pointed and said, "They said they would kill me if I didn't do as I was told. I'm not one of you. I can't defend myself."

"I'm sorry you got mixed up in this, doctor. Unfortunately, it was for nothing. You saw what I wanted these two to see. I would have rather kept you out of it," Julian said.

Clarke grinned and fired a shaft of energy at the doctor. His scream of pain reverberated around the chapel.

"Clarke," Julian said. "Still playing the fool for your master?" Clarke fumed, but refused to rise to the bait.

"I must say, your actions in Rome were inspired," Julian said to Manning.

"I'm so glad you noticed," Manning said.

"You were the puppet master and Cardinal Luciano played his part well. All the while he never knew he was the ultimate puppet. He stole millions from the Vatican Bank – a bank overseen by you. You in turn embezzled a billion or so while Luciano's thefts proved a distraction.

"Of course, you played Fr. Soski and me. We were set up to kill Luciano or be killed by him," Julian said.

"You killing him and him killing you would have been the ideal outcome, but you escaped me," Manning said.

"You are here for the Book?" Julian said as he raised his eyebrows and looked expectant.

"The Book would be an excellent place to start our discussion," Manning said.

"Of course you know the answer," Julian smiled and said and shook his head. "I'm afraid I can't accommodate you this time."

"You are so predictable, Blessing. You are not a man who would let such a treasure out of his possession. It appears we will have to force it from you," Clarke said.

"Manning's shadow speaks," Julian said and relished the way Clarke bristled.

"Oh, I was not in the shadows when that priest friend of yours died. You just mentioned him, what was his name?" Clarke asked. "I was not in the shadows when I set fire to your little hobbit either. The entire shire will miss him. In any case, I rather enjoyed that one especially."

"Fr. Marek Soski was the priest in Rome," Julian said. "Finbar Clancy was the other gentleman, a very gentle man in his own way," Julian said.

"Everyone has a signature Clarke, a presence. It is an essence that lingers. Some can detect it. You of course cannot. Your senses are dull because you have killed so often," Julian said.

"Because you like it, each kill clings to you," Julian remarked. "It defiles and overruns every cell of your body," Julian said. "That you don't remember your victims doesn't surprise me."

A part of his mind thought of kind and giving men who had their lives taken. A part of Julian never lost its focus on either

Manning or Clarke. No breath they took, no slight movement went unnoticed.

"So your death will be a part of me? How charming," Clarke said and smiled his plastic smile.

Clarke's weakness is his arrogance, Julian thought. Attack that and he will make mistakes. He need only make one.

"You needn't worry about that. Manning here pulls your strings too, so you are of little importance. My business is with him. He is strong enough to kill me. Maybe. But long before that happens you will be dead," Julian goaded.

The gates of the stone communion railing were missing. Julian passed through, turning his back on Manning and Clarke. Julian's senses were at the highest state of alert. The slightest change in either of his enemy's signatures and he would know it.

He approached the tabernacle. At his touch, the doors opened and Julian removed a cloth wrapped package. He descended the altar steps, crossed the sanctuary and returned to the communion rail.

Julian rolled back the cloth and set the Jesuit Book on the railing. His fingertips caressed the leather bound volume. He could feel the words. The thought struck him like a thunderbolt. "The ultimate source of power is the Book," he whispered. Each protector of the Book had left his stamp. They were there. They were with him.

He thought of those who had gone before him, those who gave up their lives to protect this Book. His time had come. "For you Marek and all the others," Julian said.

"What am I to do with you two?" Julian said without inflection as he turned to face his opponents. "It isn't like you will be arrested. You are beyond the reach of the law. Not above it though. There are other laws for you and me." His whisper echoed throughout the chapel. This would be a battle that would not stray outside the confines of this sanctuary.

A ball of searing energy erupted from Clarke's hand. With laser precision it made its way toward Julian with terrifying speed. Julian smiled, moved his right hand and the ball passed to one side. It was a maneuver he had practiced hundreds of times with Finbar.

"If that is the best your lapdog can do, Manning, call him off and have him lie in the corner," Julian sneered.

Manning laughed and clapped. "I must applaud your bravado if nothing else. Are you sure you would not like to join me? A man like you would be useful," Manning said as a bolt of electricity rocketed from him directed at Julian.

The heat pushed ahead well in advance of Manning's strike. Again, Julian moved his hand and the energy dissipated. It had been a powerful charge to be sure, but Julian was gathering strength from each attack.

Another charge emanated from Manning at twice the intensity of the first. It was impossible to dodge away. Julian turned it and redirected it toward its source. The charge pushed Manning back and left him gasping.

Manning had met many opponents, but there was something different now. Julian was approaching this battle from an altogether different perspective. His parries were slow and elegant, his stance and manner relaxed. Something was amiss. Manning was parrying his own attacks. He was at a loss to understand how it was possible.

Clarke erupted in a furry of white hot energy. Again, the charge seemed to fall short and disperse around Julian.

At Manning's next attack, Julian moved two steps to the right along the altar railing toward the Book. The energy seemed to evaporate before reaching him. Manning and Clarke attacked in unison knocking Julian to one knee. He rose, smiled and began an attack of his own.

For each move, there was a counter move from Julian waiting. He moved, turned aside or absorbed each attack. Manning and Clarke were wheezing for breath. Julian used the moment to erect a shield.

Manning's counterattack was fast and expert. He pushed back Julian's wall, throwing him violently into the communion railing and onto the floor.

Julian could feel it. Manning was reaching out with his mind. Julian sent out a pulse that changed Manning's focus and made the older man curse.

Julian's actions were reflexive in the exchange that followed. The Jesuit Book had seeped into every fiber of him. Every cut and thrust was parried with near surgical precision and an economy of movement.

Manning and Clarke were shocked by the skill Julian demonstrated. Newfound skills rarely overcome experience. Julian's opponents demonstrated that with a blistering array of attack and counterattack strategies.

Julian exhaled completely, then filled his lungs as he gathered the energy around him. He stood and a ball of white hot energy found its target. Manning's dark suit was smoldering from the aftershock of energy. Some of the superheated force scorched the left side of his face.

The electrical charge Clarke directed at Julian should have killed him. The offsetting energy flow from Julian caused Clarke's attack to go off target. It exploded a part of the altar, turning the ancient Irish oak to kindling.

With far more attacks than defensive moves, Manning was holding his own. For his part, Julian could feel Manning weakening. Still, he was a dangerous enemy.

All three men were panting with the effort of assaulting and defending. Julian felt it before a slight movement at the back of the chapel caught his attention. His mouth twitched into a smile.

He could feel the force around Clarke rising. Just before the point of discharge, a ball of energy scythed through the air from the back of the chapel. Julian felt the presence clearly.

Manning turned as the energy struck Clarke, knocking him to the ground.

Standing at the back of the chapel stood a small, permanently rumpled old man. "Clancy," Manning hissed before turning to face Julian.

Clarke struggled to rise, fell and struggled again. Using the wall for support, he stood and turned unfocused eyes toward his attacker.

"Ah, Mr. Clarke, burning me little house down was not a'tall a nice thing to do. That I was in the house at the time, I found particularly vexing," Finbar said and shook a finger at Clarke. "Now you and I are going to sit out this dance while these fine gentlemen transact their business."

Clarke sneered and raised an attack too late. The air went electric. Finbar transmitted a course of energy that hit Clarke in the chest and knocked him down again. Again he rose, but his left arm hung uselessly at his side and blood trickled from the corner of his mouth.

"You're a slow learner," Finbar said. "Let me tell you something, son. Move again and you'll be paying a lot less for those custom made suits of yours since they'll only need one arm." Finbar crossed his arms over his chest, leaned against the chapel door and smiled.

"Carry on with what you were doing, lads," he said to Manning and Julian. Finbar motioned for the doctor to join him. "Don't let me interrupt you two. Doctor, come sit by me, why don't you?"

Manning's face became a mask of hatred. Energy crackled around him and Julian smiled again.

The words of the Jesuit Book rang in his head. *"Let the power, the energy of life, move through you. Harness all the energy around you. Channel it from the earth and air, from everything and from nothing. Use every source, good and bad, wise and foolish that presents itself as it presents itself. Then you will know,"* the Book said in Fr. Soski's voice.

Julian was feeding off each of Manning's attacks, absorbing energy from every source. What he took from Manning was weakening his opponent while strengthening Julian.

Manning released his charge of energy, only to have it hit another absorbent barrier Julian erected. The wall began to buckle, but held.

A weak bolt of electricity emanated from Clarke. Julian reversed the charge's direction to its source at the same time Finbar struck. Clarke crumpled to the stone floor and did not move again.

Enraged, Manning struck out at Julian with a furious array of attacks and Julian's parries were just as skillful. All the while, he continued to build his store of power.

Julian's thought was powerful to the point of being painful. *"Manning, before you die, remember those you have killed and maimed."* Julian moved slowly, inexorably toward Manning. His mind raced, considering and reconsidering, weighing and balancing options for the best attack.

Manning, with feral reflexes, struck when he believed Julian's mind was focused on Clarke. The attack was sharp and sustained, but deflected by a confident, powerful, and ready Julian.

The attack on Manning was well thought out. It was as relentless as Julian's forward steps. As he advanced, his assaults transformed and forced themselves into Manning's every fiber. The room hummed with the energy signature of each man.

Revenge. Justice. Death. Those were Julian's thoughts, his motivation. "But not by my hand," Julian whispered to himself as he wiped blood from the corner of his mouth with the back of his hand. And smiled.

Advance, attack, faint, counterattack. Julian's advance on Manning was unremitting, focused, driving, merciless. Each attacked a different weak point, then shifted and picked another.

Manning was no less formidable. His attacks and counterattacks were ferocious. Each move calculated to inflict the most amount of damage to mind and body as possible.

Julian was hurled over a set of pews. He rose coughing blood. He gained his footing as Manning unleashed a firestorm of raw, unrestrained, soul-battering energy. Julian absorbed the energy he could and deflected what he could not. He moved from one pew to the next, supporting himself as he reeled.

The veins in Julian's neck distended and his breath came in short gasps. He turned his eyes to Manning's face. He only had one thought.

"Not today," Julian hissed as his world went white. His attack was stunning in its complexity. Julian watched Manning's face as it went from incomprehension to a black rage. Electricity crackled and stung. The chapel moved between near darkness and blinding light. Deafening, exploding, parried, dissipated, absorbed balls of energy moved around the building like lightning.

Julian continued to close on Manning. His was a hatred-fueled vehemence, his face a map of malice. Julian wanted to be as close as possible when his opponent succumbed.

Manning was thrown against a set of pews, picked up and thrown again. His senses were muddled. His eyes were taking longer to focus after each attack. He knew his mind was yielding under Julian's assault.

Julian glanced at Clarke. The man hadn't moved and there was very little signature left. Manning used that moment to strike with everything at his disposal. The room went alive with rippling, high voltage heat. Thrown over the communion rail, Julian hit the sacristy floor hard. Dazed, both men knew they would not be able to withstand another offensive. They lay panting, unable to focus for several moments.

Julian struggled to gain his footing and stood. Weakened, he remained iron willed. He felt Manning's icy fingers close around his mind. The pain was agonizing, blinding, and draining the life from him.

Julian closed his eyes and as he opened them, he could see only one thing – Manning.

Finbar, Clarke, the doctor, all were gone. All that existed was a narrow, silent hallway leading straight to Manning. Julian felt Manning build one last burst of energy, one last attack. Julian's discharge of energy sliced the air in a band of pure white heat.

The exchange threw each man in the air and against opposite walls of the chapel. Both tried to rise. Both tried to gather the last of the energy that animated each of them.

Julian's arms and legs were numb and didn't answer his commands. He slumped back against the cool stone wall and rose again. He could feel his mind straining, trying to maintain some semblance of self while holding Manning off.

Manning lay crumpled against the far wall. He felt the edges of his mind failing after Julian's assault. He knew the full force of Julian's attack would come hard and fast. Manning's had to come faster.

He struggled to his feet and saw Julian unprotected and exposed. Dragging his leg and leaning to one side, Manning approached Julian.

Enraged, Manning struck out with an array of savage attacks. Julian's parries were still adroit but weakening. All the while he continued to rebuild his store of power.

"Let's end this," Julian said his mouth twisted into an ugly sneer.

"I could not agree more," Manning replied before releasing a vast cascade of raw energy.

Julian pushed back, strengthened by the electrically charged chapel. Attack, attack, attack, parry, attack, riposte, attack. He was relentless, driven by a thirst for justice for his friends. The attacks left Manning gasping for air.

He released a scorching attack. Julian intensified it many fold and turned it back on itself. The force brought Manning to his knees, his eyes blurred, his mind blank.

Julian reached out. The Jesuit Book rocketed toward him and into his left hand.

Out of reflex, Manning sent the energy back out to destroy Julian, only to have it hit a protective wall and bounce back. 'Walls within walls,' the Jesuit Book had said.

In a millisecond, Terrance Patrick Manning was obliterated by his own hand. The searing heat twisted into fire and reduced him to ash.

* * *

# Chapter Twenty-one

Julian limped to the communion railing. He set the Jesuit Book on stone worn smooth by countless supplicants. He looked at the Book and his gray eyes softened. "There is only one way to protect you from the world," Julian whispered. He held out his hand and the Book burst into flames. It flared, turned to a pure blue flame, and died out. Only shards of the leather cover and a scorch mark on the railing remained.

Julian turned to the front door and said to Finbar, "Where is Clarke?"

"He made it out the side door in all the confusion," Inspector Flannigan cut in as he descended the stairs from the choir loft.

Finbar's eyes moved to where Clarke had been. "My guess is he is far from here licking his wounds. We'll save him for another day," the old man said.

"Inspector," Julian said, "I must say you're not all that good at following my directions."

"I would have to disagree. You said don't interfere and interfere I did not. If you wanted more you should have mentioned it," the inspector said and smiled.

"I had a few things on my mind at the time. I will have to remember to be more precise with my suggestions going forward."

"Oh, admit it, boyo," Finbar said. "The lad caught you out." The old man's eyes were alive with mischief.

"In any case, you didn't interfere and that was good," Julian said and continued. "Kevin, you wanted to understand. Well, now you know the reality of evil.

"I suspect you are going to have to do some extensive explaining. You can pretty well assume your superiors won't want a paper trail on any of this though. The less written down the better. You are now the resident expert on all things, let's just say, unusual. That should make you as popular as the plague and as useful as its cure."

"What was that book? Whose was it?" Flannigan asked and nodded toward the altar railing.

"Oh that?" Julian smiled a melancholy smile. "Just a book a friend loaned me. No one I know ever truly owned it and now no one ever will," Julian said and looked to the spot where the Book had burned so brightly.

"Julian, your friends from Rome, how are they? Still with you?" Finbar asked.

"No, they gave me what energy they had and went on their way," Julian said.

Finbar looked thoughtful and smiled. "Time for you to go home, my friend."

* * *

Sean drove while Julian rode shotgun and Finbar stretched out on the back seat of the patrol car. The drive from the monastery to Cappel Vale had been long, but uneventful.

The exit from the M1 highway was easy to miss and Sean did. He drove another mile before making an illegal U turn. Julian thought of the first time he walked from the M1 to the village of Cappel Vale.

It seemed a long time ago. He wondered if it was possible to go home. Much had happened to change him.

The patrol car mounted a rise in the road and slowed to a stop. Sean turned off the engine. The only sound was Finbar's soft snoring.

"Julian," Sean said. "Oi was wondering, would you mind walking to the village from…"

"Maher, why don't you tell Julian what you've done?" Finbar said.

Sean turned around but Finbar-of-the-maniacal-grin was out of reach.

"What have you done this time, Sean?"

"Why can't you go back to the village, Maher?" Finbar giggled.

"Oi swear to you ya little worm, Oi will kill you one of these days," Sean hissed.

"Julian, old son, what do you suppose a peeler could do that would get him exiled from his own beat?" Finbar asked.

"The question hasn't changed, Sean," Julian said. "What have you done?"

Sean made a study of the instrument panel and said nothing.

"Finbar, you are unusually well informed, it seems. Why don't you tell me what he's been up to?"

"Well, I am glad you asked," the scruffy little man began.

"Finbar!" Sean hissed.

"It seems the local representative of the Gardaí decided Cappel Vale was in need of some excitement. To accomplish this, he managed to set neighbor against neighbor, brother against brother, etcetera," Finbar grinned.

"How did Sean manage that?" Julian asked. His voice was mild and he tried not to laugh.

"Well, my spies tell me the eejit Maher set a pack of witches on various of his enemies. He followed this by telling each of said enemies it was all the work of another of his enemies. Are you following all this?" Finbar said.

"Who was caught up in this brilliant scheme?" Julian asked.

"He snagged Moira Hagan a bit, Tom Cahill quite a bit, all the pub owners, a monumentally stupid thing to do by itself, the Hackett sisters and a few others of no particular note. That is to say, everybody else in the village save Fr. Fahey, the nuns and the good and lovely Dr. Dwyer," Finbar said.

"It was the doctor who tumbled to it first. When the wounded started arriving at her surgery, it wasn't long before Maher's cunning, but sadly stupid, plan came undone," Finbar concluded.

"Sean, what was it about this plan that made even the slightest bit of sense to you?" Julian asked his big friend.

"Finbar makes it all sound foolish. It started out quite simply. That shrew, Moira Hagan, needed to be taught a lesson. It was a fine plan, but it got a little out of hand in all the excitement," Sean said.

"A little out of hand, is it? A little out of hand? For the love of God, listen to the man!" Finbar wheezed between fits of laughter. "God does love a simpleton."

"Julian, please, Oi'll let you out here and you need only take a little stroll into the village. Everyone will be waiting for you Oi'm sure," Sean said.

"The entire village is waiting for you Maher. With pitchforks," Finbar hooted.

"You have to go home sooner or later, Sean," Julian said.

"It is Garda business Oi have to attend to over at Dundalk," Sean mumbled.

"That 'business' better include enlisting the riot squad to follow you home," Finbar said.

"So you want Finbar and me to hoof it into the village while you skulk off and wait for things to blow over. Do I have that right?" Julian asked. "I don't know if I should enable you. Aiding and abetting, no?

"I just have another question. When all of this becomes known to the Gardaí, what plan do you have in place for that?" Julian asked.

"Find out is it?" Finbar cackled. "No one in the village will ever say a word. They would rather hoist poor Sean's guts on a stick. Isn't that right, Maher?"

"Please, Julian, Oi'm begging you, please. Just do this one thing for me and Oi'll be indebted to you forever. Oi'll name my children after you. All six of them."

"Well, that would be pretty confusing and wouldn't please your wife a bit. Tell you what I'll do. As you say, Finbar and I will walk the rest of the way. Somehow we will figure out a way to smooth this over," Julian said.

"Do you think you could?" Sean asked, the gleam of hope and gratitude hot in his eyes.

"Can't promise anything," Julian said.

"I'll promise you something, Maher," Finbar said. "To be sure, our man Julian is a smooth rascal and if anyone can get you out of this, he's your man. However, your missus and Moira Hagan will not be pacified in the slightest, so you have that to look forward to," Finbar hooted.

* * *

"You look especially lovely today, doctor," Bridget said.

"Aye, she tarted herself up nicely," Moira added. "A special occasion, lass?"

Ailís Dwyer took one last look at herself in the mirror over the fireplace. "I have no idea what you are talking about. I understand Sean Maher is due to return today. I can think of nothing else, beyond his warm reception, that would be of any note."

"It will be quite a bit hotter than warm, I can tell you," Moira said and her eyes narrowed while she grinned at thoughts of murder and Sean Maher.

"That, however, is not what we were referencing. I understand Mr. Maher is returning Julian to us," Bridget said and smiled her most charming smile.

"Oh, he is returning? I hadn't heard and wouldn't have cared less if I did," Ailís said, attempting to sound cold.

Bridget and Moira had to look at the floor to stop from laughing.

"Mama! Mr. Julian and Mr. Clancy are coming up the road," Timothy Dwyer said and ran out the door banging the screen behind him.

Ailís turned too quickly, and took a step before she regretted it and tried to cover her excitement. "I will have a talk with Timothy about opening and closing doors properly."

"Perhaps, like his mother, he was just overly enthusiastic at the prospect of Julian's return," Bridget said and sipped her tea, while Moira tucked into her Irish whiskey infused bread and butter pudding.

"Although you seem to be, I certainly am not interested in the comings and goings of Mr. Blessing."

Loud shouts, laughter, greetings, applause and generalized carousing erupted in the street. Standing in her parlor before the cold fireplace, Ailís drew in a quick breath and held it as perspiration beaded on her forehead and her hands began to shake.

Moira leaned over to Bridget and whispered, "He'll never tumble to it and I've got a fiver that says so."

Bridget pursed her lips then grinned. "Done. Five Euros," she whispered. Moira put out her hand and the ladies shook on it.

"Mama, Mr. Julian asks if you would join him on the front porch," Timothy shouted as he entered the house.

"First of all, we do not yell in the house. Second, if your Mr. Julian wishes to speak with me, he should knock and state his business. Otherwise he can go away."

"But mama, he needs to see you real bad and said to bring the ladies too," Timothy said and nodded to Bridget and Moira. Bridget looked at the floor while Moira hid her smile behind her hand.

"But mama, you have to hurry!" Timothy began.

"But nothing. You tell your Mr. Julian that I am not in the habit of…" Ailís began.

"Timothy," Bridget slid in smoothly, "please tell Mr. Julian we will be along momentarily and shall not keep him waiting long. Please close the door quietly on your way out."

"Of all the gall!" Ailís said louder than she intended.

"Yes, of all the gall," Moira chimed in. "Have I not put up with weeks of your mooning and whining all over the place? Was it not you who told me you begged your god to bring Julian back to you? Has not every villager and bumpkin within twenty kilometers been to see me to repeat your sad song? And for you to stand there looking all regal with your 'couldn't care less', now that takes real gall!"

"My darling Ailís, enough of this charade. It has fooled no one including you. It is time we go and welcome Julian. He has returned and is waiting."

"And," Moira added, "repair your lipstick. Gnawing on your lower lip has worn it off. You look lopsided."

Moments later, Bridget glided out the door followed by Moira. The screen door slammed shut. A full minute passed, but no Ailís appeared.

"I must compliment you on those red slippers," Bridget said to Moira.

"Do you like them? I think they are very fetching. A bit tight, but they will stretch in time," Moira said.

Another minute passed and no Ailís.

"Girl, don't make me come in there and get you!" Moira hissed.

After another moment Ailís emerged. She was wearing taupe slacks, an off-white silk blouse and a stern expression. Julian stared and swallowed hard. His Ailís, she looked exactly as she had when he first met her on his arrival in Cappel Vale.

Ailís' expression dissolved at the sight of the entire village, including visiting witches, standing at her front porch. The sound of sudden applause was deafening.

There he was, the man she had prayed would return to her. She drove her fingernails into her palms and bit the inside of her cheek to keep her emotions in check.

It was as if Julian drew a breath he thought might never come. Seeing her was enough to raise his heart rate and quicken his breathing. He smiled, the smile turning to a look of concern and then to a grin.

Moira cocked an eyebrow and the crowd fell silent.

"I've missed you so much," Julian said and dropped to one knee.

"Ailís, I have been to Dublin to see your parents. I have asked your father for your hand and he was kind enough to give me his blessing. Your mother has taken to calling me 'son,' which I think is rather sweet," Julian began.

"Asked for my hand? My father? Gave you his blessing? Who is he to be giving away my hand. Is this the middle ages? My mother, mind you, calling you son," Ailís began. "Either you are lying or they have gone senile since I last saw them." Ailís backed up to a safe distance.

It was obvious she would draw no closer than ten feet, so Julian moved to her. Again, he knelt and took her hand, but she managed to wrest it away from him. "I don't know what you think you are doing, but…"

Julian took her hand again, drew a breath and closed his eyes. This time she felt a slight electrical charge course up her arm. She tried and tried again, but could not move her arm or hand.

"Ailís Dwyer, will you be my wife?" Julian asked.

"I wouldn't have you on a bet and…" she began. The rest of what she said was lost as the crowd erupted into applause before it was silenced by a look from Bridget.

"Uh, a moment if you would. Before you complete that sentence as you might like right now, please think of the consequences," Julian interrupted.

"Consequences? Did I hear you correctly? Are you threatening me or have you gone as mad as my parents?"

"Not a threat, my darling," Julian whispered as he stood and released her hand. "Never that. It is just that if you refuse me, Fr. Fahey and the sisters will be greatly disappointed in you, your parents will be mortified and the village will be scandalized. That doesn't even begin to address the torments Timothy will suffer."

"So, it is that important you think you are, Mr. Julian Blessing. Refusing you would bring ruin upon me. Is that it? Am I understanding you?" Ailís demanded. "You arrogant bastard."

"Ladies don't say, 'arrogant bastard,' my dear, even when confronted by one," Bridget said and smiled.

"Well then, I'm obviously not a lady," Ailís said and the venom dripped from her voice.

"I am certainly not that important, but you are; both of you," Julian answered.

"You are too right. Timothy and I are that important and too good for the likes of you, mister comes-and-goes-as-he-pleases," Ailís concluded in a huff.

"Dearest, indeed, you're right. I should have come to you and explained, but…" Julian began.

"Too right you should have. You were stubborn, self-centered and arrogant," Ailís said.

"You are right. I was stubborn, self-centered and arrogant," Julian said, but was cut off.

"And pigheaded," Ailís added.

"Yes, and pigheaded, but my love, we are getting very far off the point," Julian began again.

"I wasn't talking about Timothy," Julian said. "I was thinking of the two of you." He reached out his hand with infinite care and set his palm on her stomach.

"Take your hands off me. You dreadful, deluded man. Two of who? What are you talking about?"

Bridget held out her hand and Moira quickly filled it with a five Euro note. "I've never been so happy to be wrong. He has come a long way," Moira whispered as she stepped up next to Ailís.

"Been feeling a bit queasy when you lift your pretty head off the pillow in the morning? You complained to me about back pain recently. Have we been a bit more fatigued and cranky than usual? Headaches, is it? Pardon me saying anything, but your usually well-turned ankles look a bit thick just now," Moira said. "You're a doctor. You figure it out, my fine colleen."

Ailís stood open mouthed as her head became a beehive of signs, symptoms and timing. "No. It isn't possible. It can't be. I took steps, precautions. I was just off my normal cycle. We took precautions. No, I tell you. It isn't possible."

Julian placed his hand on her stomach again. "Now will you marry me? I really want to make an honest woman of you and to give our child my name, but you are making it difficult."

Ailís dropped her chin to her chest and sighed. To the wild cheers of the crowd she said, "I suppose so."

"Could you put a little enthusiasm into it?" Julian asked.

"What a peculiar man you are," Ailís said. "Of course I'll marry you, ya eejit."

"That's more like it. See, it wasn't so hard now was it?" Julian asked.

## The End

# On behalf of the author and Penman House Publishing, thank you. We appreciate your support.

Reviews are the life's blood of publishers and authors and help inform other readers. They act as signposts on the literary landscape.

Please take a moment and leave a review of this book on Amazon, GoodReads or wherever readers gather.

**About the author:**

K. Francis Ryan's experience as a feature writer for a small town newspaper, a police officer and an internationally accredited stockbroker is evident in the writing of the Echoes Quartet, a paranormal mystery series set in the present day.

**Other books from this author:**

Echoes Through the Mist – Book I in the Echoes Quartet Available Now

Julian Blessing's high-octane Wall Street career is likely to land him in prison. The economy is rapidly melting down. His ex-wife wants him dead and some Russian mobsters share her sentiments. And that's just today.

Julian thinks now would be the right time to start listening to the voice only he hears. The words Julian hears bring a message as emphatic as it is baffling and propels him to a village on the rugged coast of Ireland.

A madman possessing supernatural powers wants to sow terror in the hearts of those in the village. His craving for revenge and his limitless greed put Julian directly in his path. By protecting the village, Julian puts himself high on the madman's to-be-slaughtered list.

Desperate for any advantage, Julian discovers the Hagan, a woman with vast supernatural gifts who is steeped in Ireland's ancient wisdom. Hers are otherworldly talents with decidedly this-worldly applications.

Victims are multiplying fast as Julian races to unlock the Hagan's mysterious arts. Her arcane knowledge is the only hope he has of drawing his fellow villagers back from annihilation.

To stay alive long enough to use what he learns, Julian must trust his heart to a stranger, his soul to a witch and place his life in the hands of a village full of Irish lunatics.

## Echoes Through the Vatican – Book II in the Echoes Quartet Available Now

A shadow organization, tracing its dark ancestry back two thousand years, wants only one thing from Julian – Assassinate the pope, the leader of 1.2 billion Roman Catholics.

A corrupt cardinal, an honorable priest, a sadistic mobster, a whorehouse madam and a stymied police inspector – They all want something and that something is Julian Blessing.

**Echoes from the Past – Book III in the Echoes Quartet Available Now**

Terrorist bombings, political unrest and a man whose life is in tatters...

Evil exists and it wants Julian Blessing dead.

Julian, a man with exceptional paranormal powers, is back in Ireland to face his most daunting challenge yet.

The Jesuit Book – it is a book that some say doesn't exist. Others are afraid to admit it does. Others will murder to get it. Julian is the keeper of the Book. His task is to protect it regardless of the risks, heedless of the costs.

During his mission to Rome, friends died and others wish they had. Badly scarred emotionally, Julian has returned to Ireland to rebuild himself as well as prepare for the conflict he knows will come. Can he overcome his own demons in order to fight those who would take the Book and his life?

**Book IV in the Echoes Quartet Coming Fall of 2017**

**Other Books from Penman House Publishing**

**By Aaron Aalborg**

**They Deserved It – Available Now-** This thriller begins as a historical novel set in 17th Century Italy, a time of superstition, plagues and cynical exploitation of young women. This ripping yarn of illicit love, hundreds of poisonings, the Inquisition, torture and witch burnings is built around true events.

**Revolution - A thriller to change the world. Available Now –** This book is an essential read for anyone who really wants to change the way the world is run. It describes a violent revolution in the United Kingdom that blossoms to upset the entire world order.

**Terminated Volume1- From the Slums to the Falklands War-Available Now –** Revelations from recently declassified government archives drive the start of this thriller in two parts.

**Terminated Volume 2-** Expected Mid 2017 – Thwarted by sociopathic colleagues and corrupt partners, Alex turns his expertise in killing to hunting down and murdering those who ruined his life.

**Cooking the Rich – A Post-Revolutionary Necessity – Available Now –** A spoof book of jokey recipes. It skewers politicians and the undeserving rich with humor and insight.

**Doom, Gloom and Despair: Tales to Horrify and Amuse-Available Now –** A collection of stories combining black humor, misery and horror. If you can laugh at humankind's self-importance and stupidity, this book is for you. If you are willing to consider wild and terrifying alternative futures, you will find it darkly entertaining.

**By Michael Crump**

**Candyman's War –** Available Now – A thriller going well beyond the genre, "Candyman's War" is narrated from within the history of the most violent civil war of the Americas.

**The Oligarch** – Available Now – The second novel of the three-part series, Los Chapin!

**By Riley Smythe**

**Eleven Days** – Available Now – A phone call takes Lela Itzel out of her familiar and safe New England boarding school and thrusts her into the turbulent post-civil war Guatemala.

*All titles are sold exclusively through* Amazon.com

www.ingramcontent.com/pod-product-compliance
Lightning Source LLC
Chambersburg PA
CBHW050028180626

46810CB00002B/629